Dear parents, caregivers, and educators:

If you want to get your child excited about reading, you've come to the right place! Ready-to-Read *GRAPHICS* is the perfect launchpad for emerging graphic novel readers.

All Ready-to-Read *GRAPHICS* books include the following:

★ **A how-to guide to reading graphic novels for first-time readers**

★ **Easy-to-follow panels to support reading comprehension**

★ **Accessible vocabulary to build your child's reading confidence**

★ **Compelling stories that star your child's favorite characters**

★ **Fresh, engaging illustrations that provide context and promote visual literacy**

Wherever your child may be on their reading journey, Ready-to-Read *GRAPHICS* will make them giggle, gasp, and want to keep reading more.

Blast off on this starry adventure . . . a universe of graphic novel reading awaits!

pocket.watch

RYAN'S WORLD

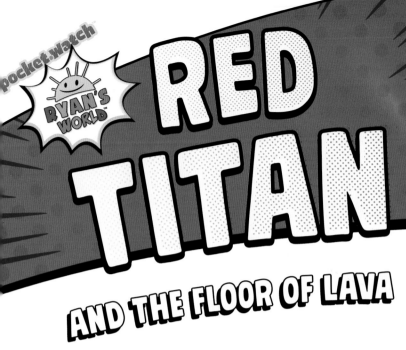

RED TITAN

AND THE FLOOR OF LAVA

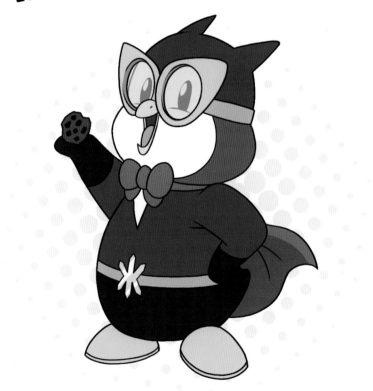

SIMON SPOTLIGHT
An imprint of Simon & Schuster Children's Publishing Division
1230 Avenue of the Americas, New York, New York 10020
This Simon Spotlight edition May 2022
Text by Arie Kaplan
TM & © 2022 RTR Production, LLC, RFR Entertainment, Inc. and Remka, Inc., and
PocketWatch, Inc. Ryan ToysReview, Ryan's World and all related titles, logos and
characters are trademarks of RTR Production, LLC, RFR Entertainment, Inc. and Remka,
Inc. The pocket.watch logo and all related titles, logos and characters are trademarks of
PocketWatch, Inc. All Rights Reserved. Photos and illustrations of Ryan and Ryan's World
characters copyright © RTR Production, LLC, RFR Entertainment, Inc. and Remka, Inc.
For more information about special discounts for bulk purchases, please contact
Simon & Schuster Special Sales at 1-866-506-1949 or business@simonandschuster.com.
Manufactured in China 0222 SCP
2 4 6 8 10 9 7 5 3 1
ISBN 978-1-6659-1359-1 (hc)
ISBN 978-1-6659-1358-4 (pbk)
ISBN 978-1-6659-1360-7 (ebook)

pocket.watch

RYAN'S WORLD

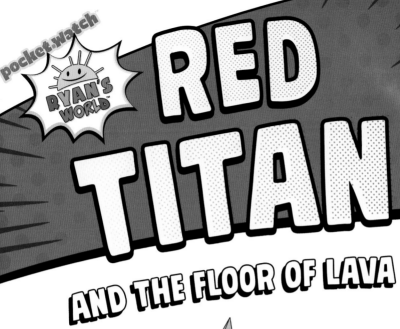

RED TITAN

AND THE FLOOR OF LAVA

by **RYAN KAJI**
written by **ARIE KAPLAN**
illustrated by **PATRICK SPAZIANTE**

Ready-to-Read *GRAPHICS*

Simon Spotlight
New York London Toronto Sydney New Delhi

HOW TO READ THIS BOOK

Ryan is here to give you some tips on reading this book.

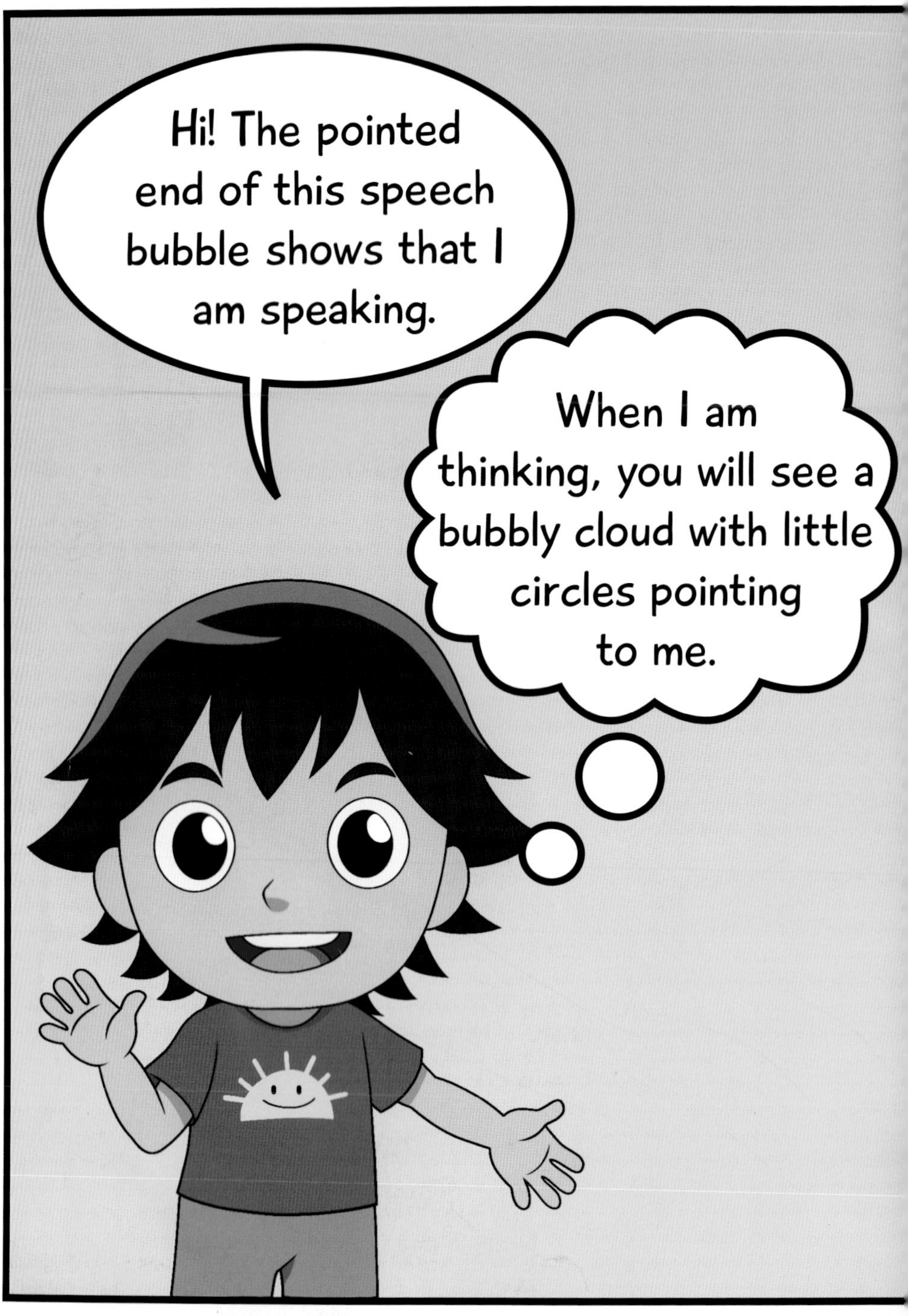
Hi! The pointed end of this speech bubble shows that I am speaking.
When I am thinking, you will see a bubbly cloud with little circles pointing to me.

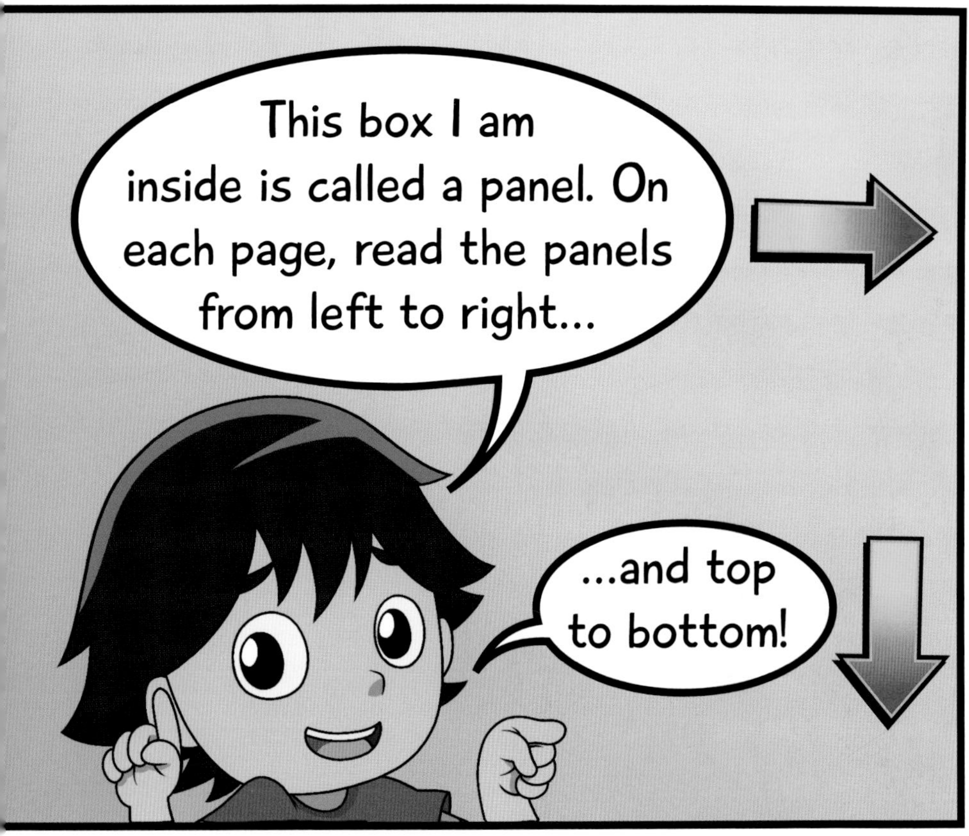
This box I am inside is called a panel. On each page, read the panels from left to right...
...and top to bottom!

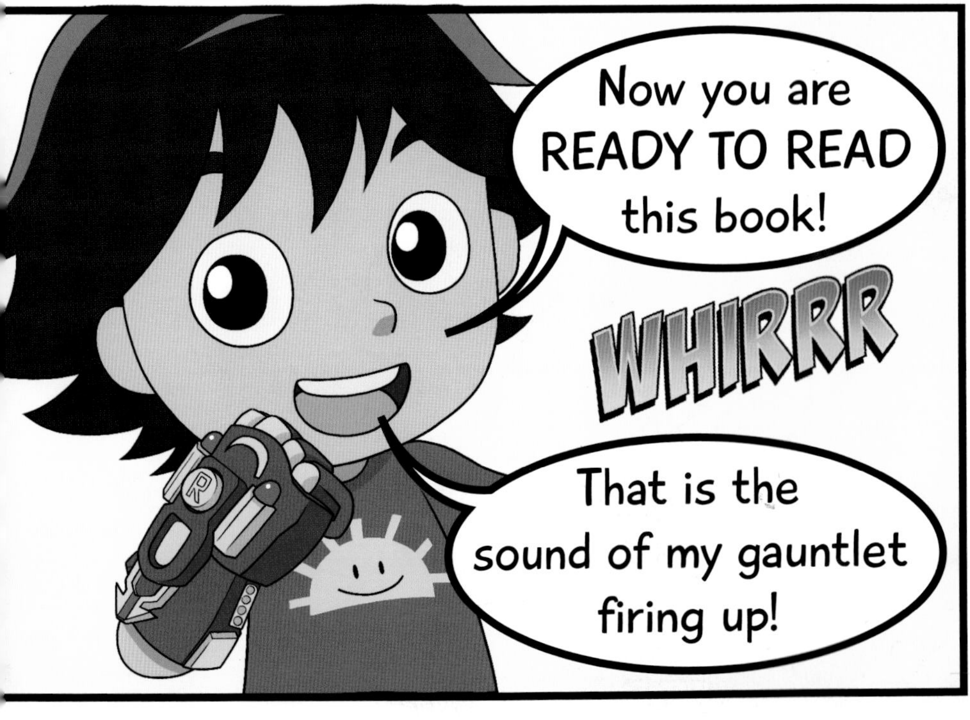
Now you are READY TO READ this book!
WHIRRR
That is the sound of my gauntlet firing up!

It was a beautiful day. Ryan, Peck, and Combo Panda were on their wa
to a picnic.

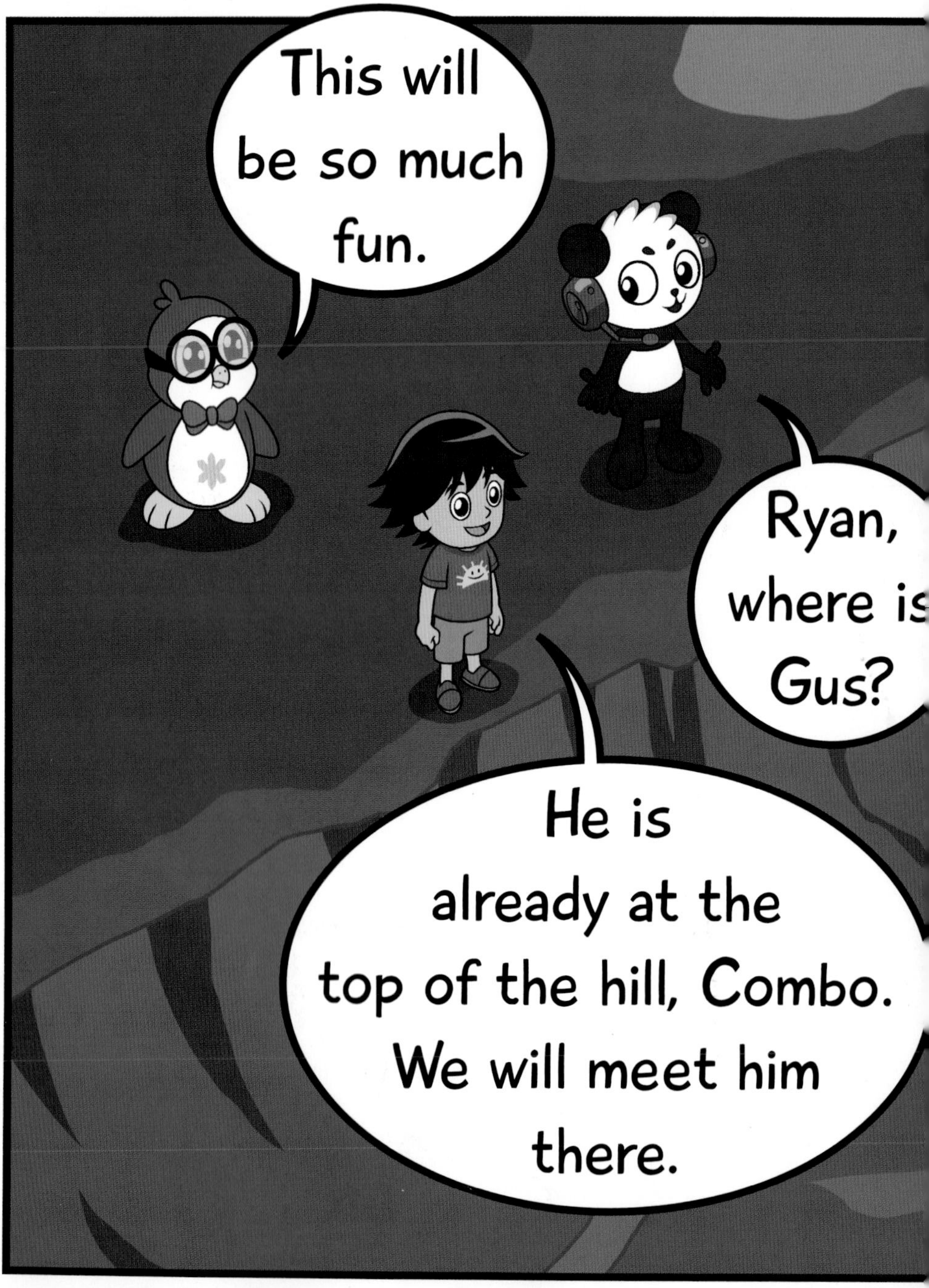
This will be so much fun.
Ryan, where is Gus?
He is already at the top of the hill, Combo. We will meet him there.

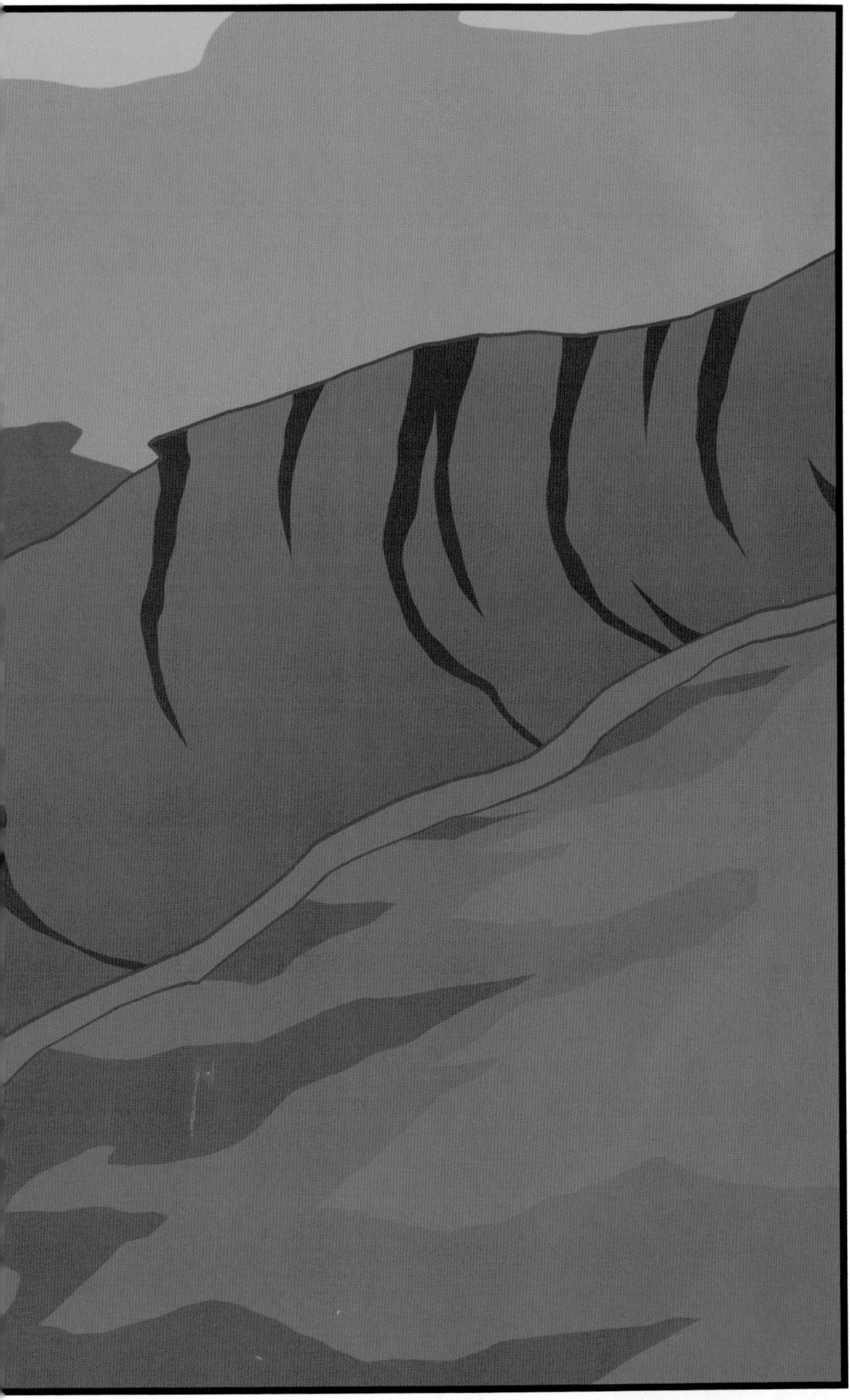

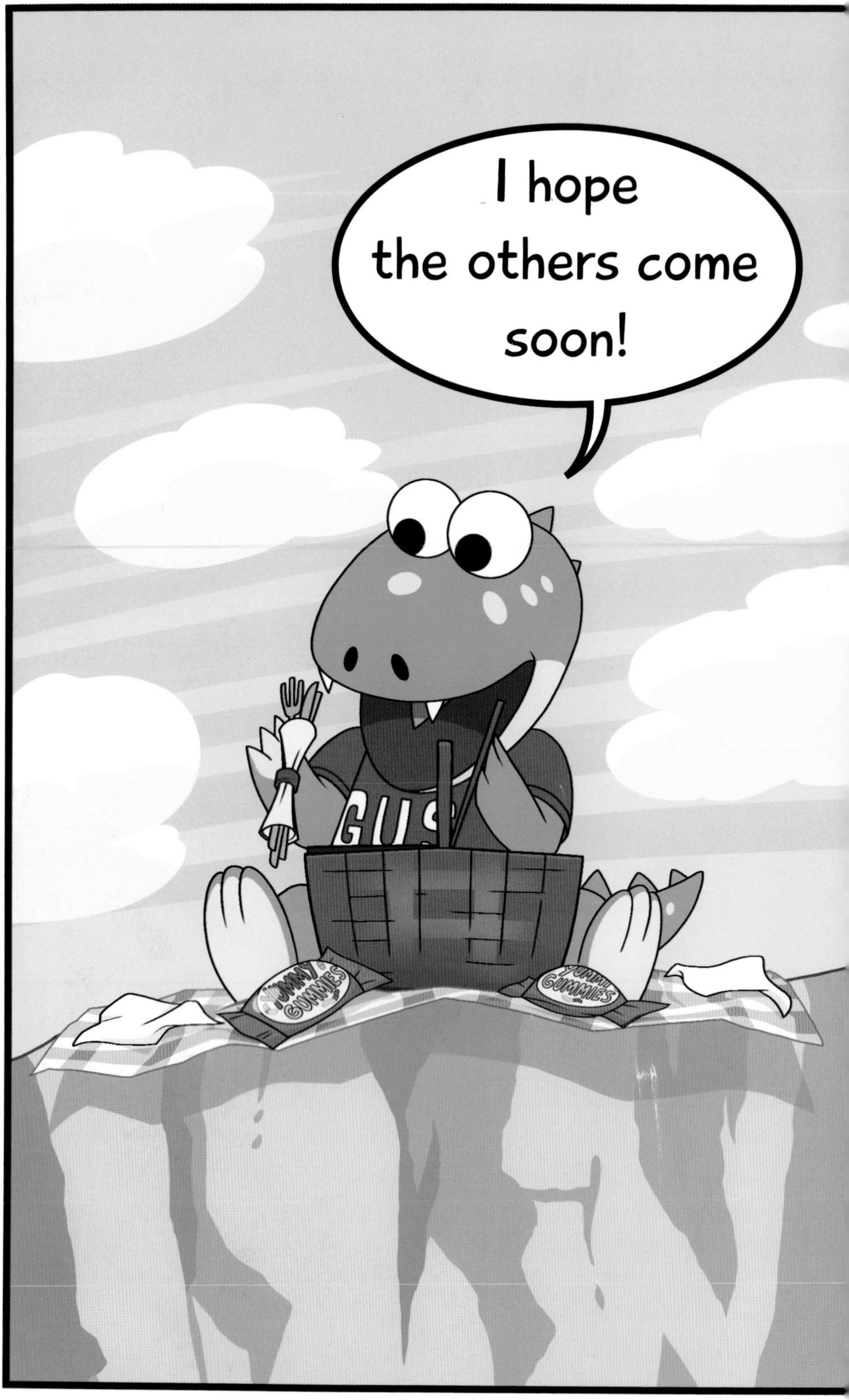
I hope the others come soon!
GUS
YUMMY GUMMIES
YUMMY GUMMIES

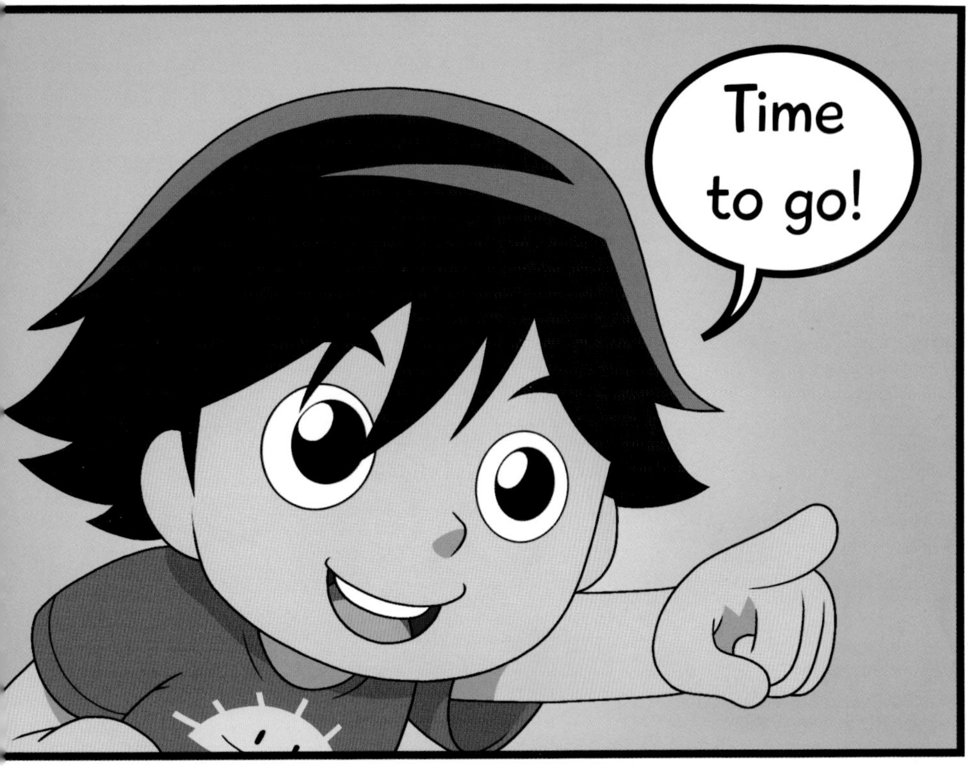
Time to go!

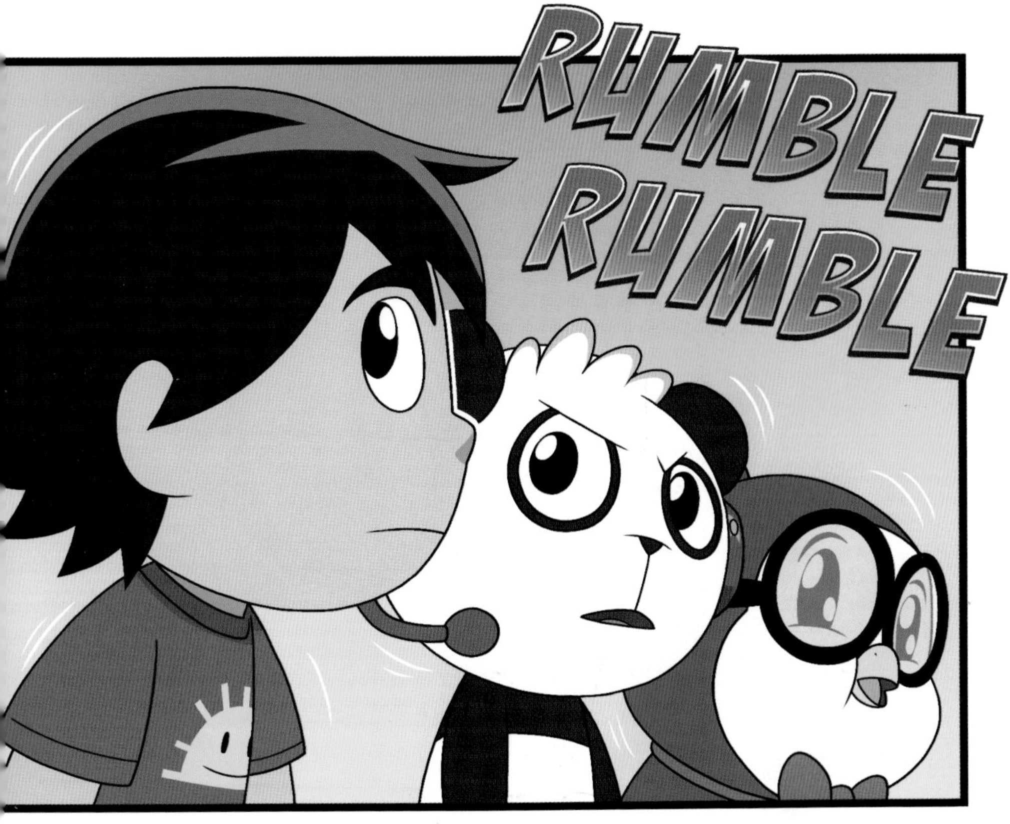
RUMBLE RUMBLE

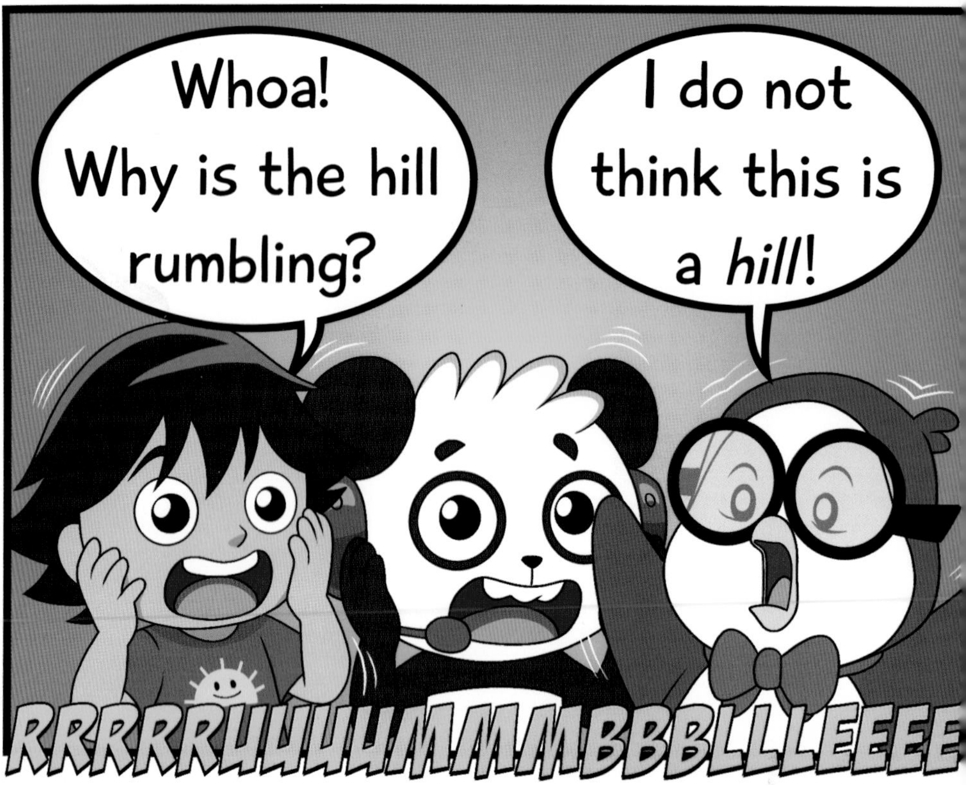
Whoa! Why is the hill rumbling?
I do not think this is a *hill*!
RRRRRUUUUUMMMMBBBLLLEEEE

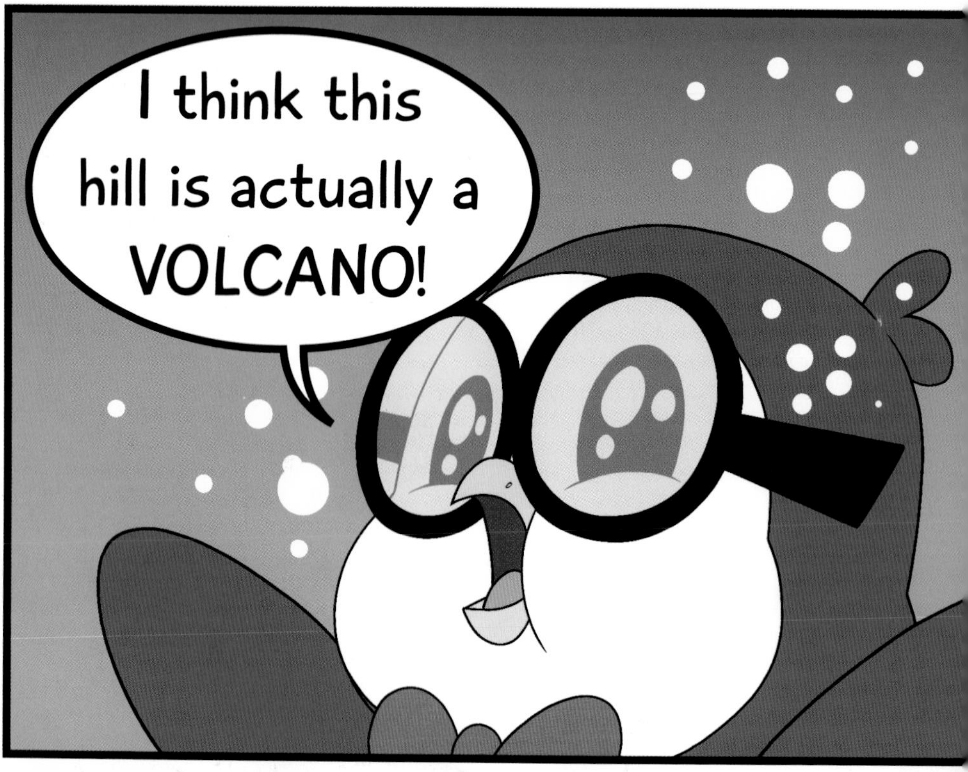
I think this hill is actually a VOLCANO!

Meanwhile, at the top of the hill...

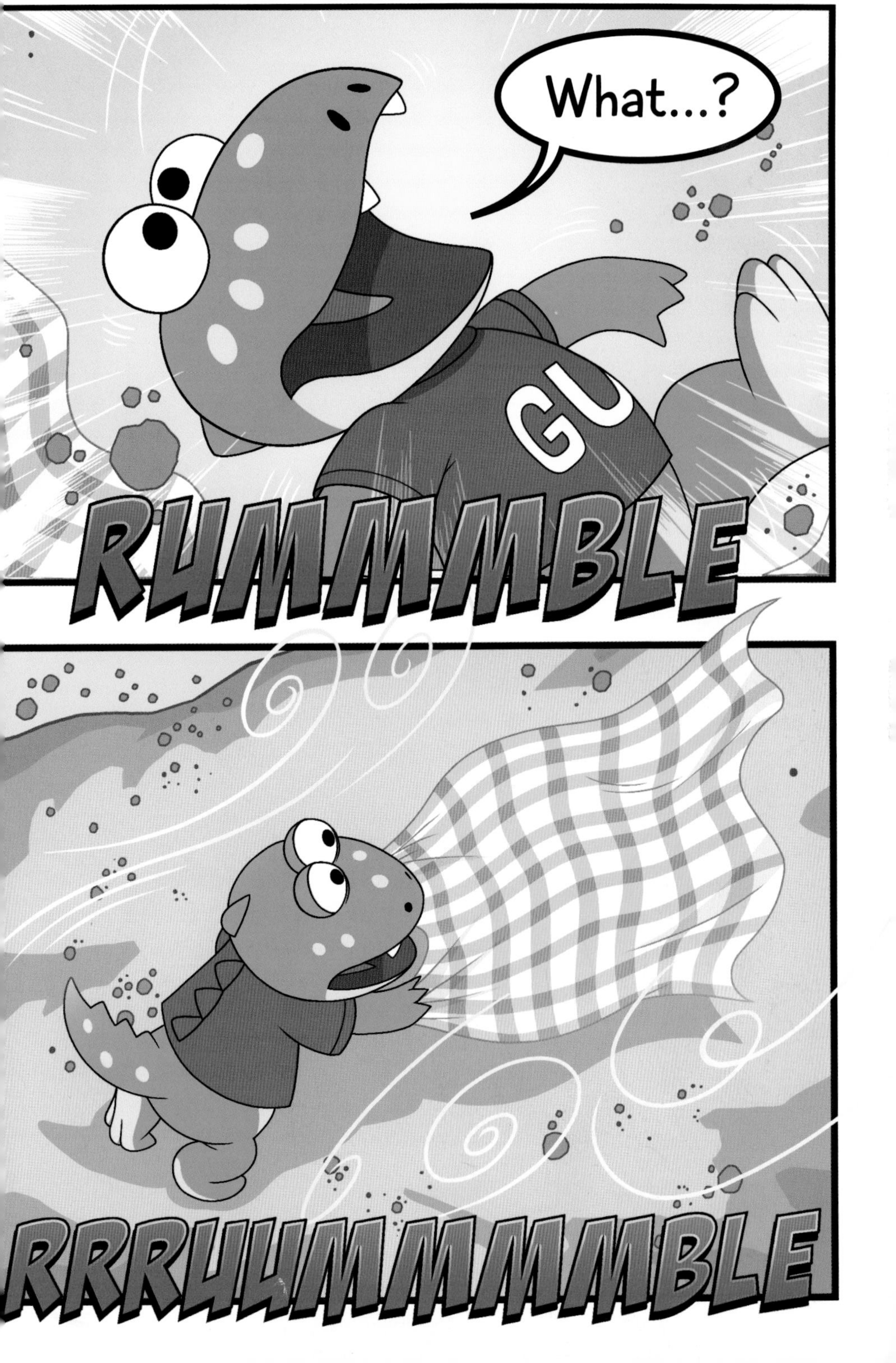
What...?
GU
RUMMMBLE
RRRUUMMMMMMBLE

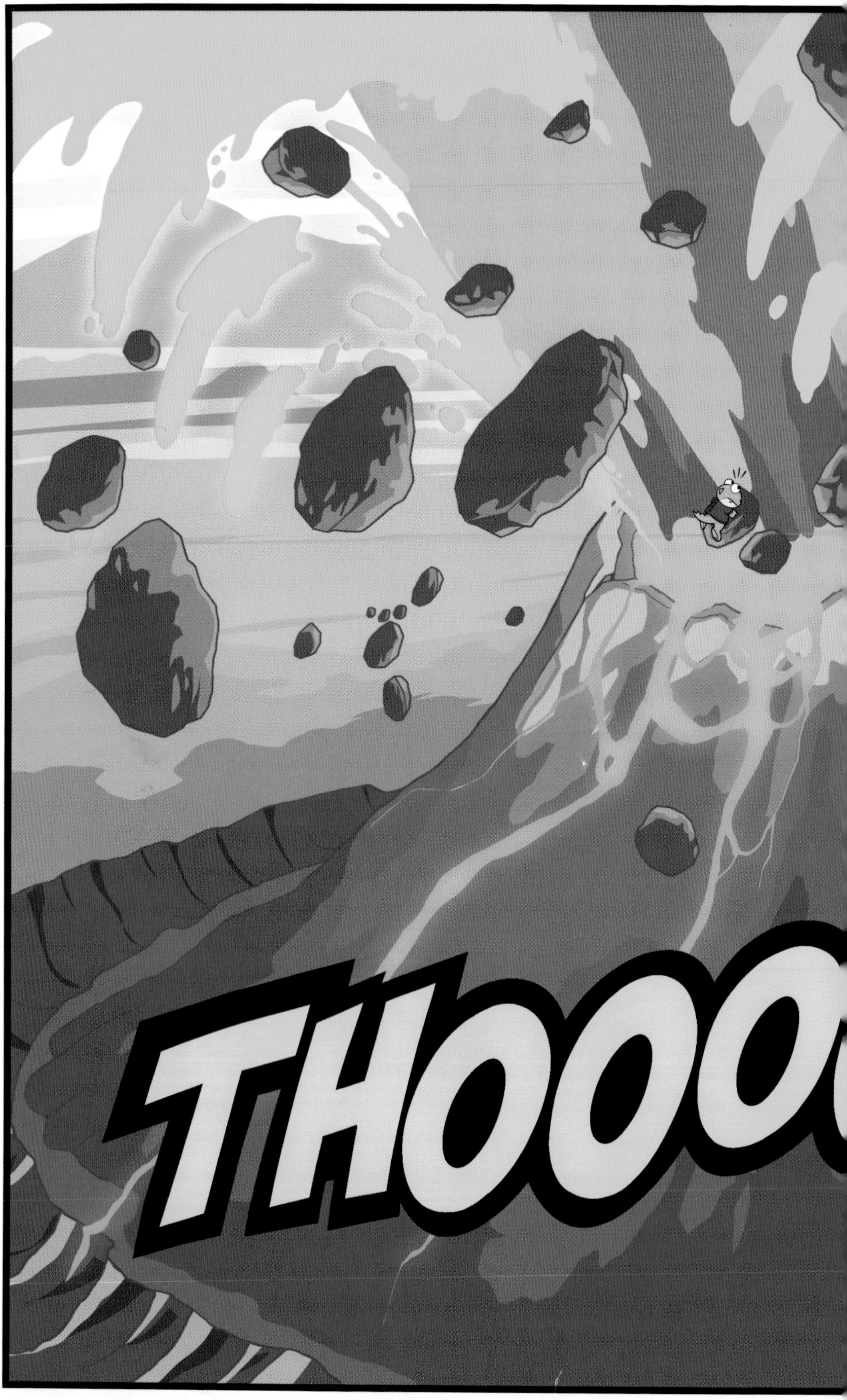
THOOO

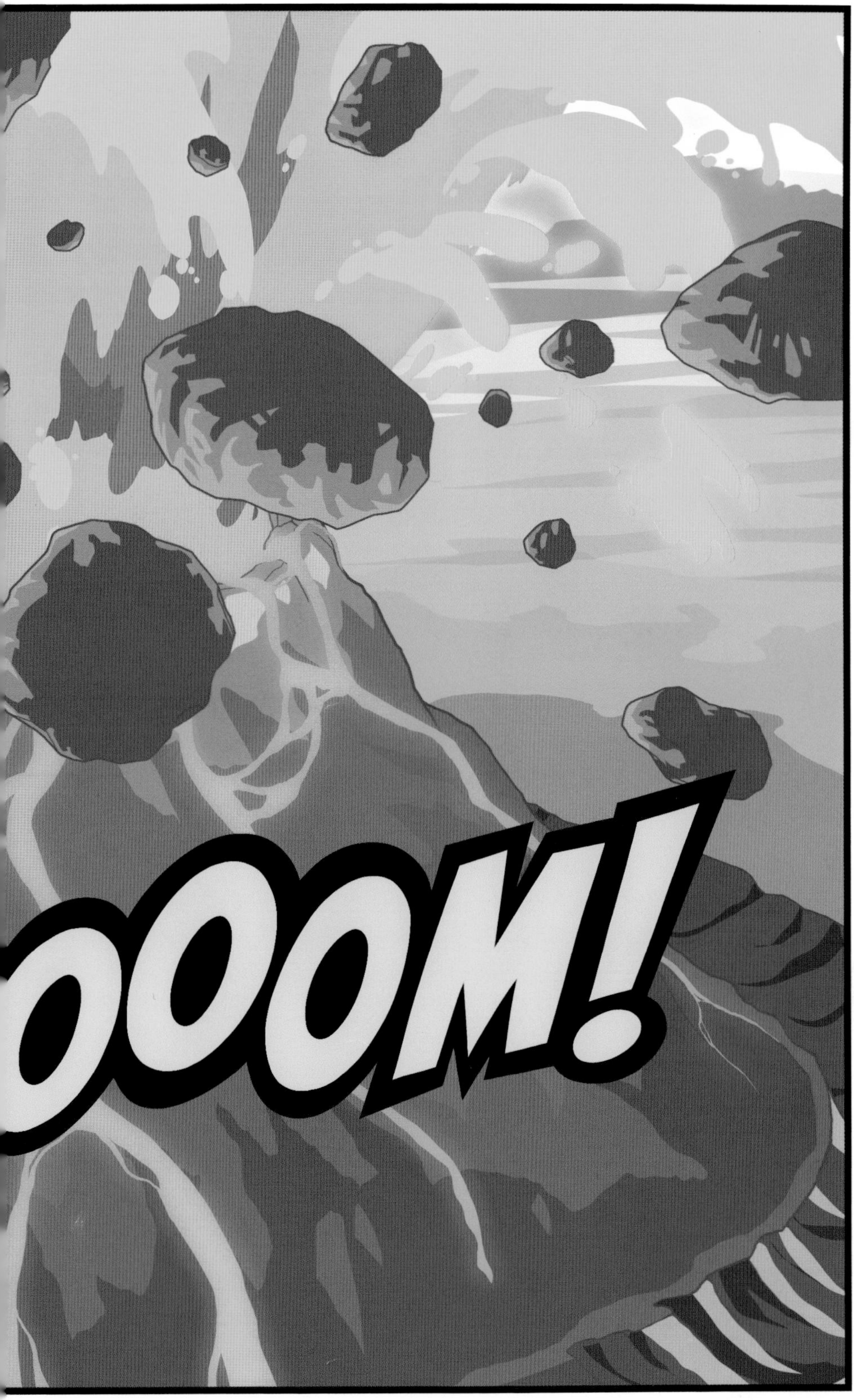
OOOM!

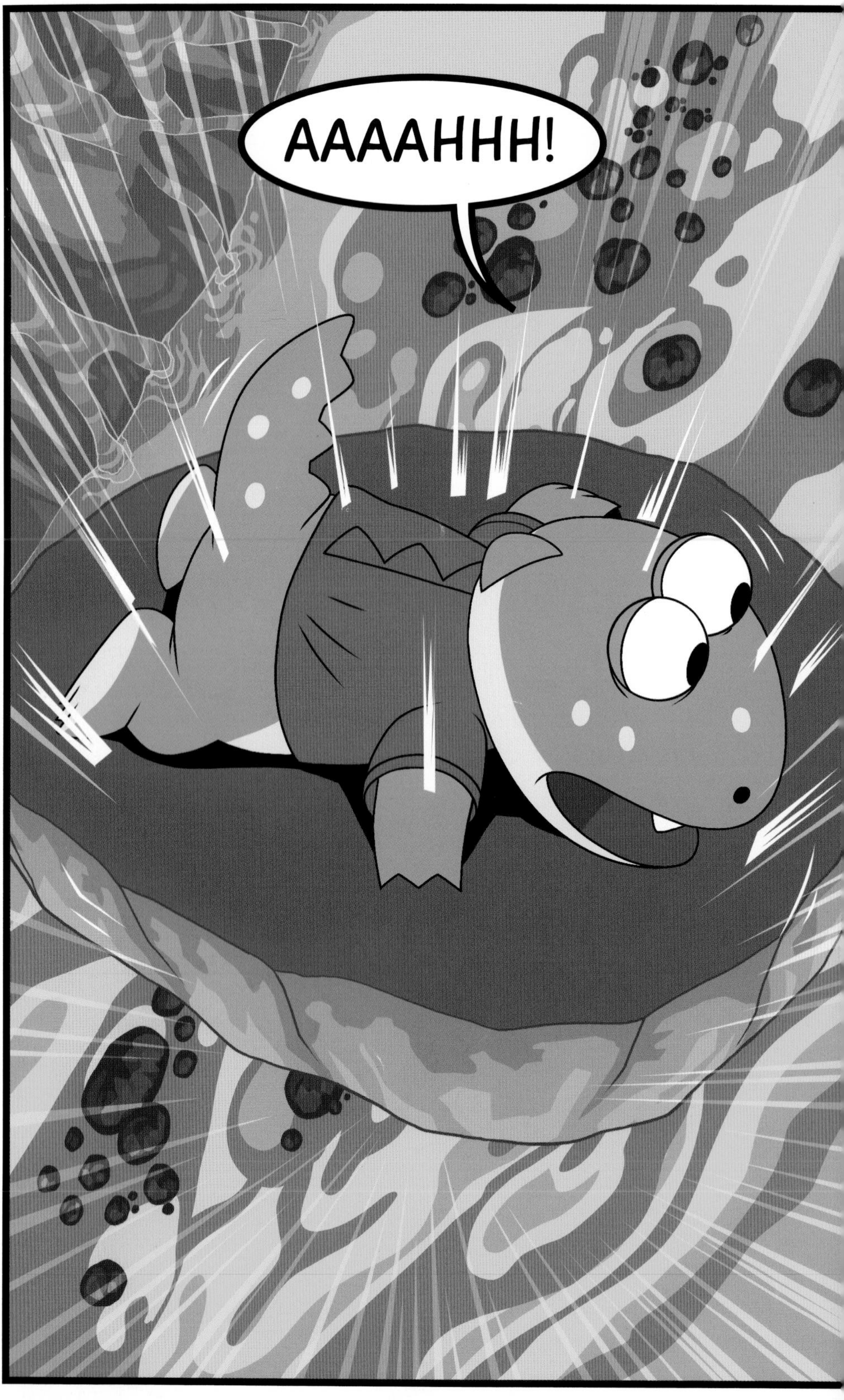
AAAAHHH!

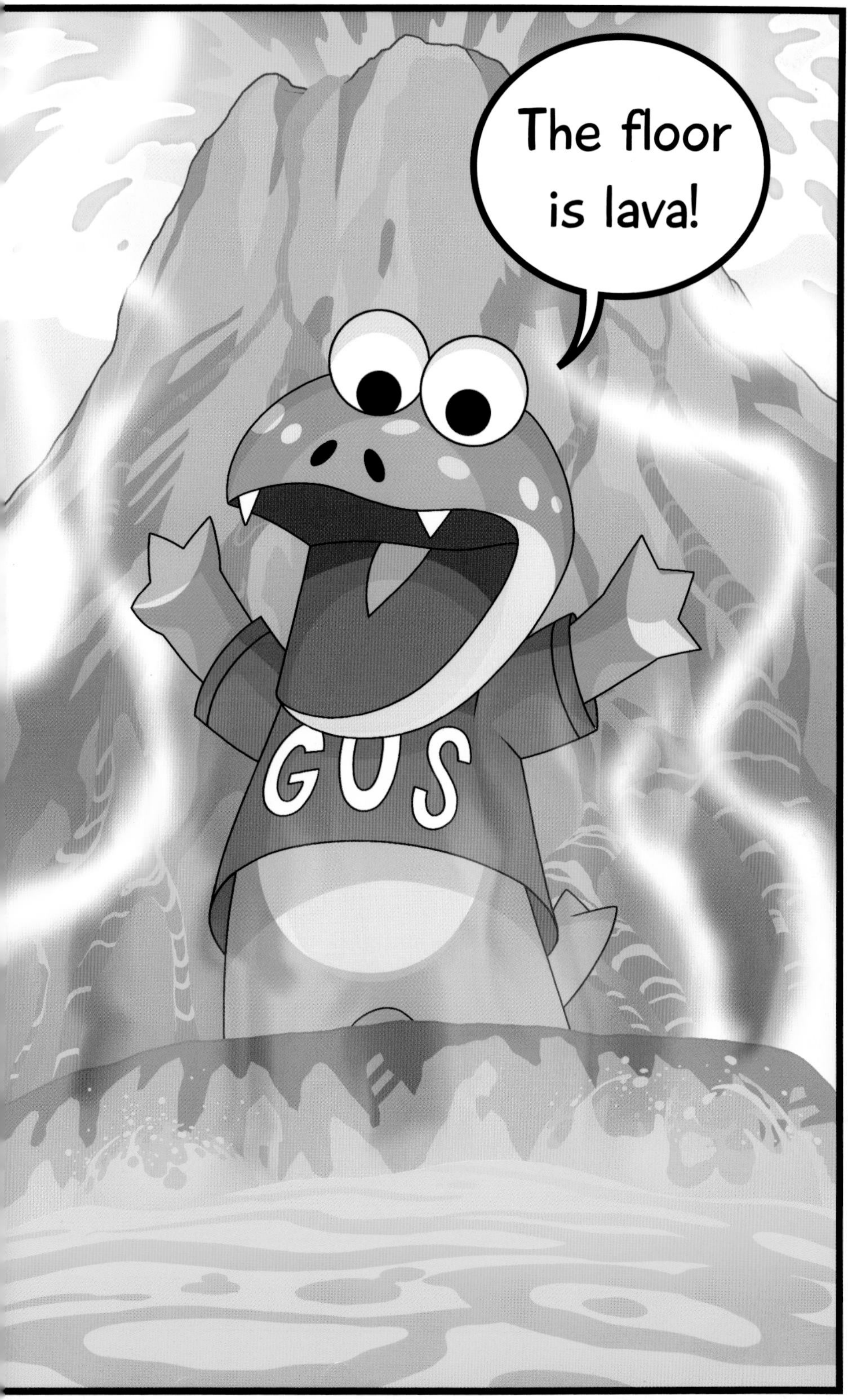
The floor is lava!
GUS

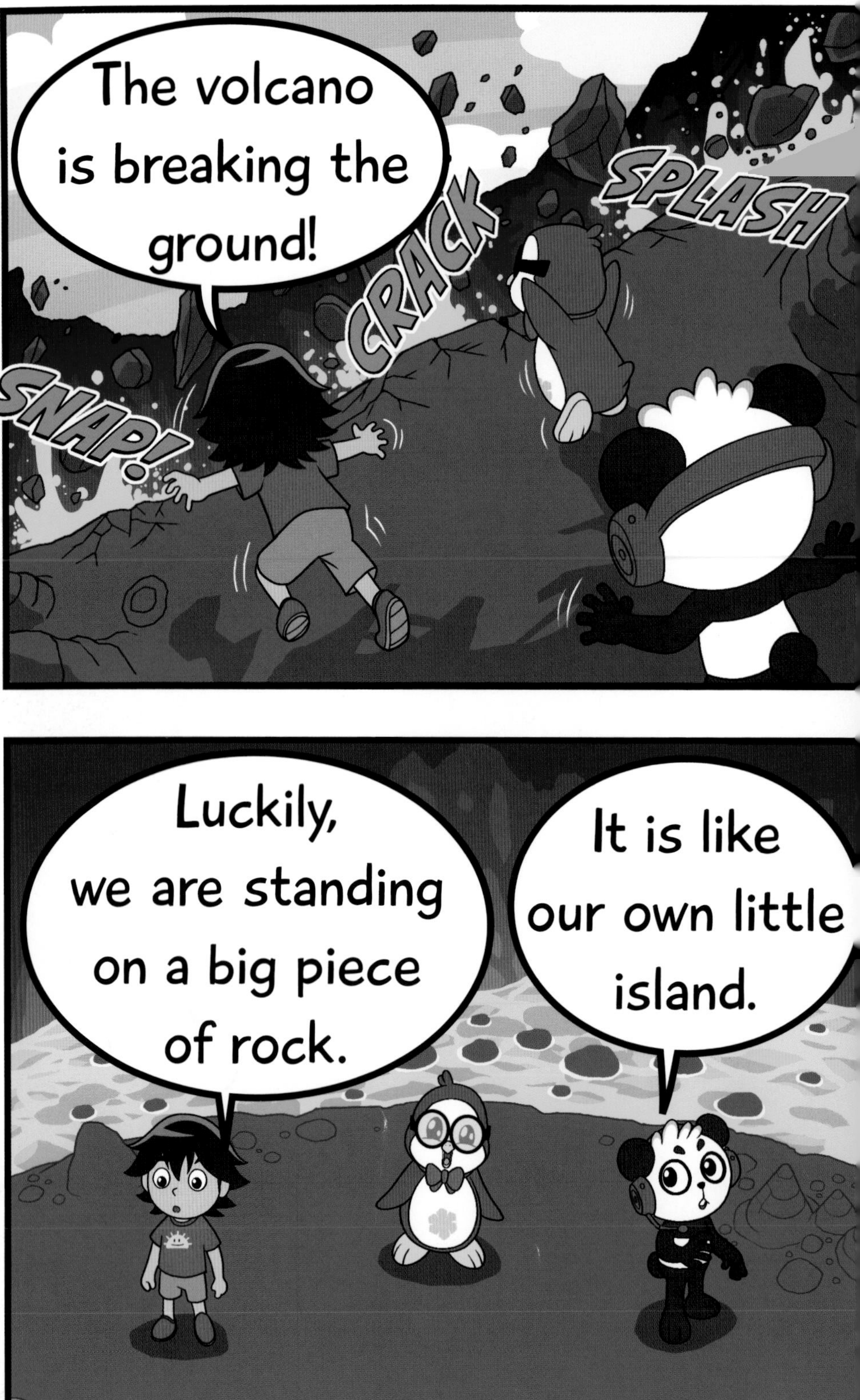
The volcano is breaking the ground!
SNAP!
CRACK
SPLASH
Luckily, we are standing on a big piece of rock.
It is like our own little island.

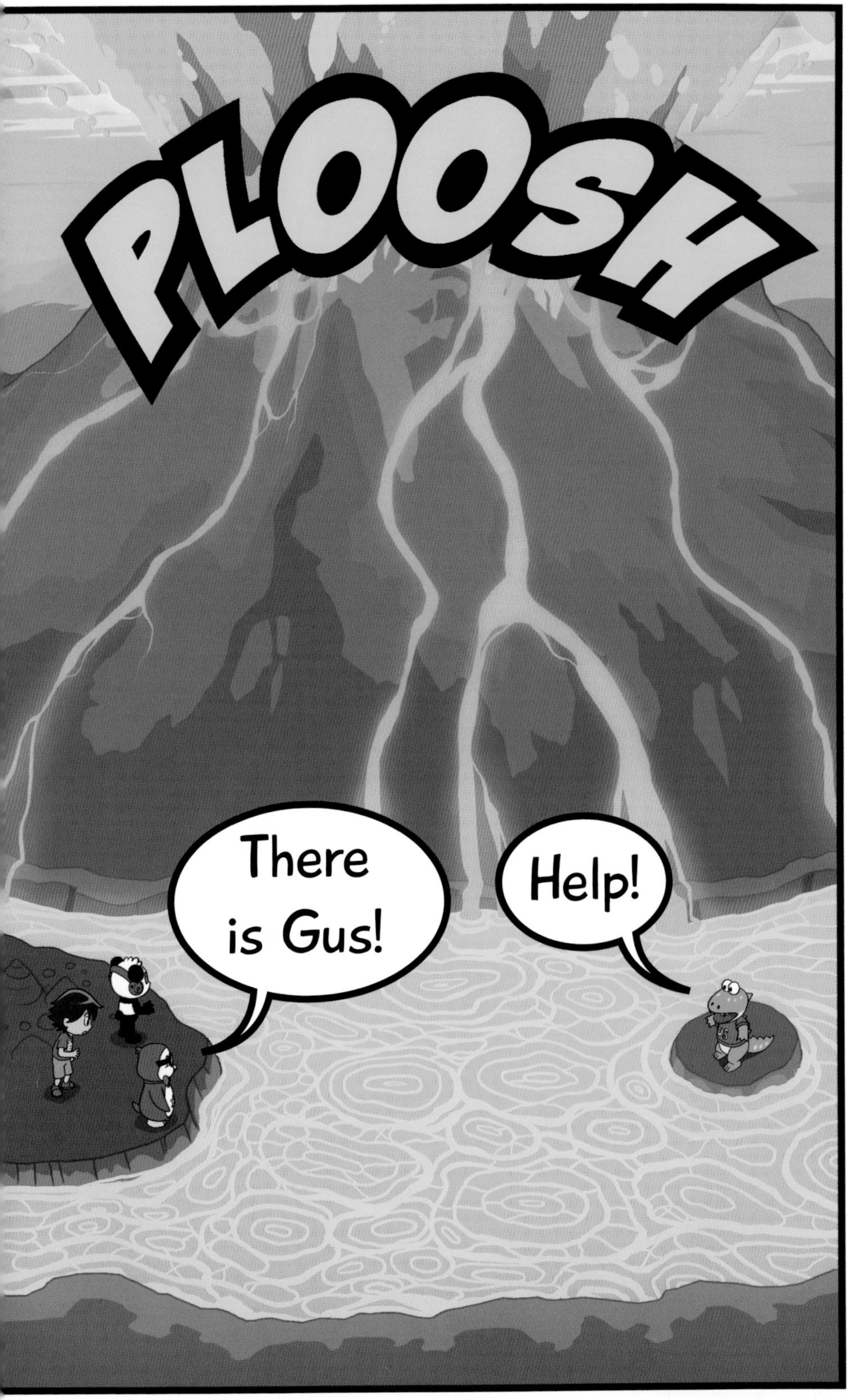
PLOOSH
There is Gus!
Help!

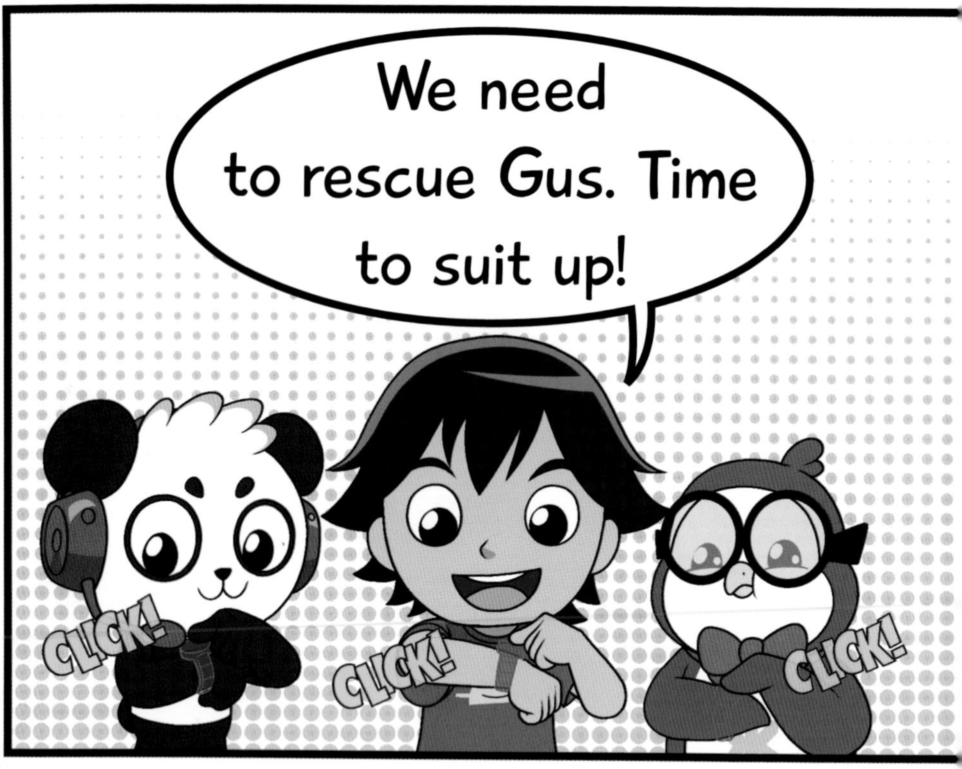
We need to rescue Gus. Time to suit up!
CLICK!
CLICK!
CLICK!

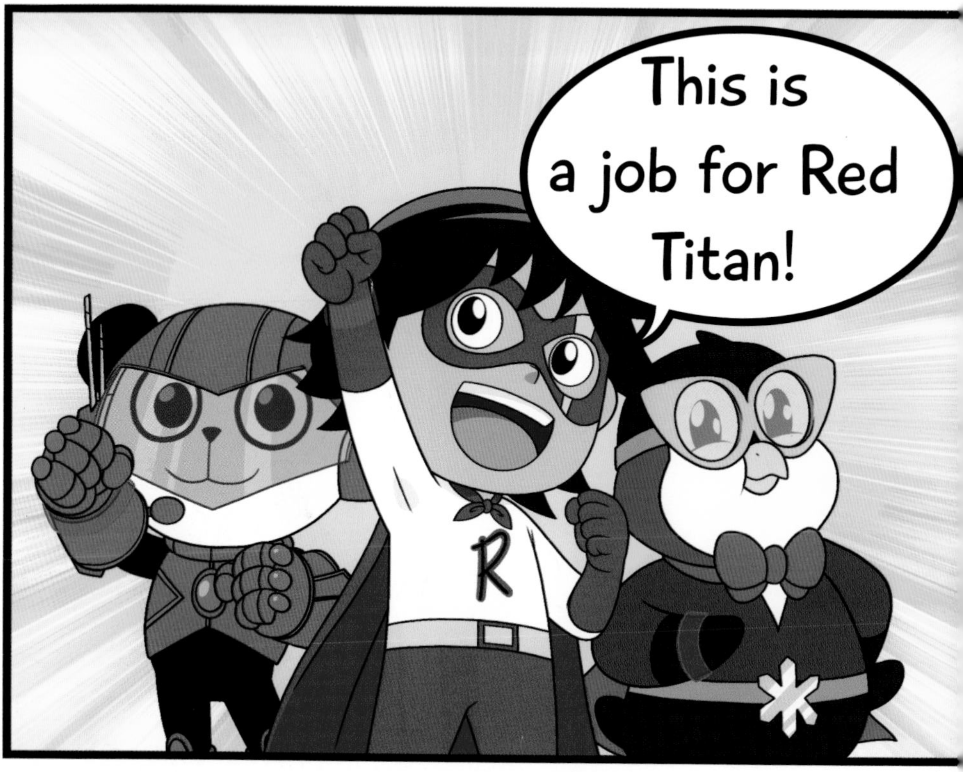
This is a job for Red Titan!
R

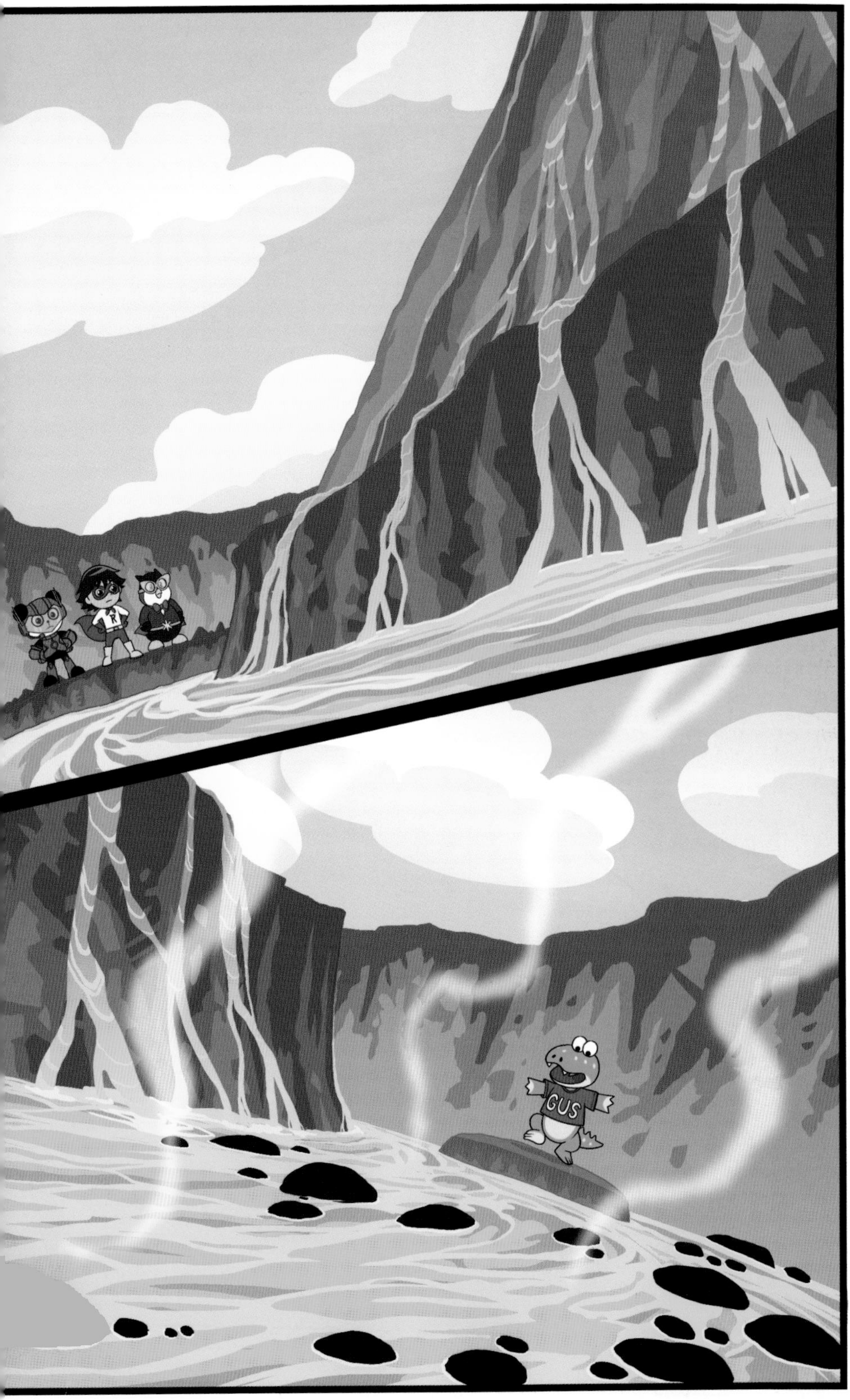
GUS

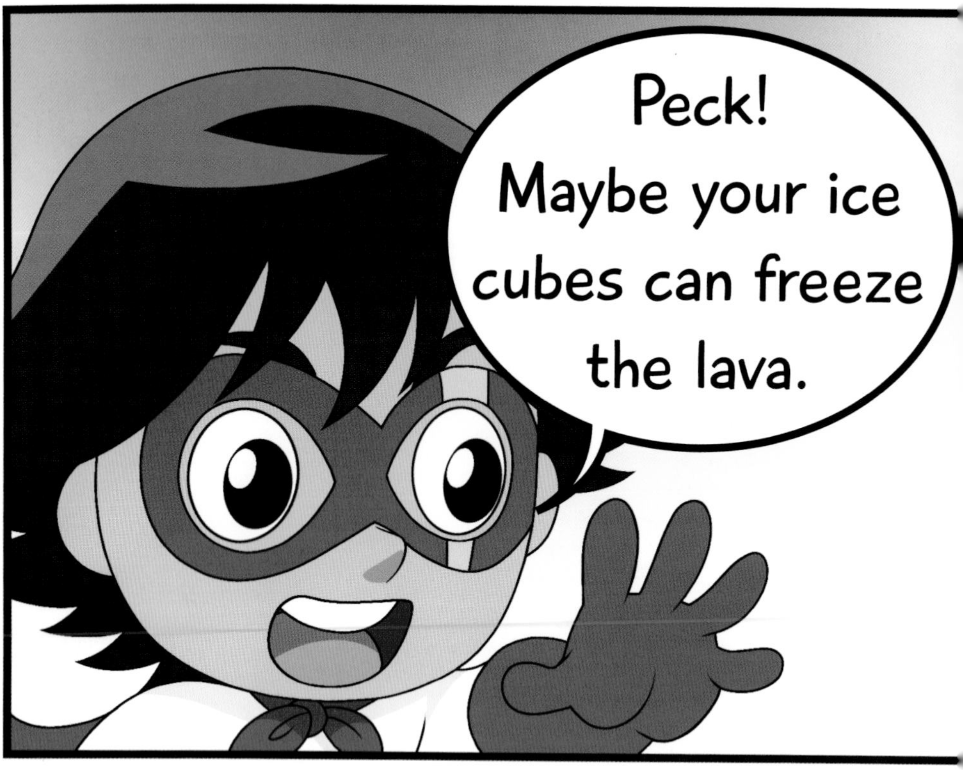
Peck!
Maybe your ice cubes can freeze the lava.

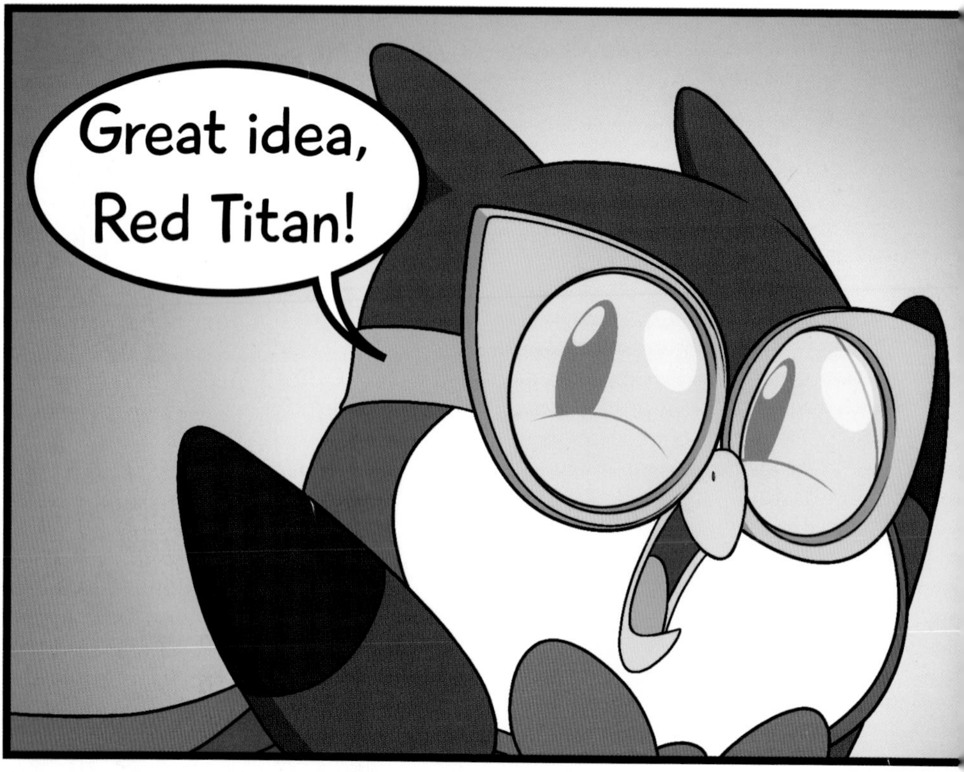
Great idea, Red Titan!

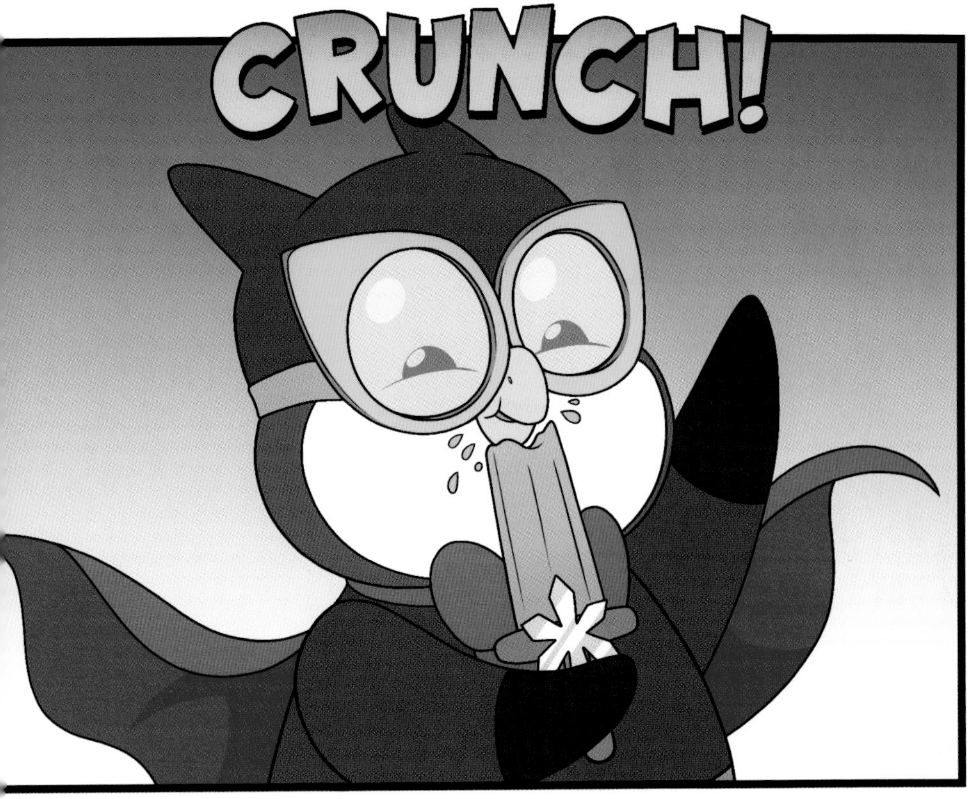
CRUNCH!

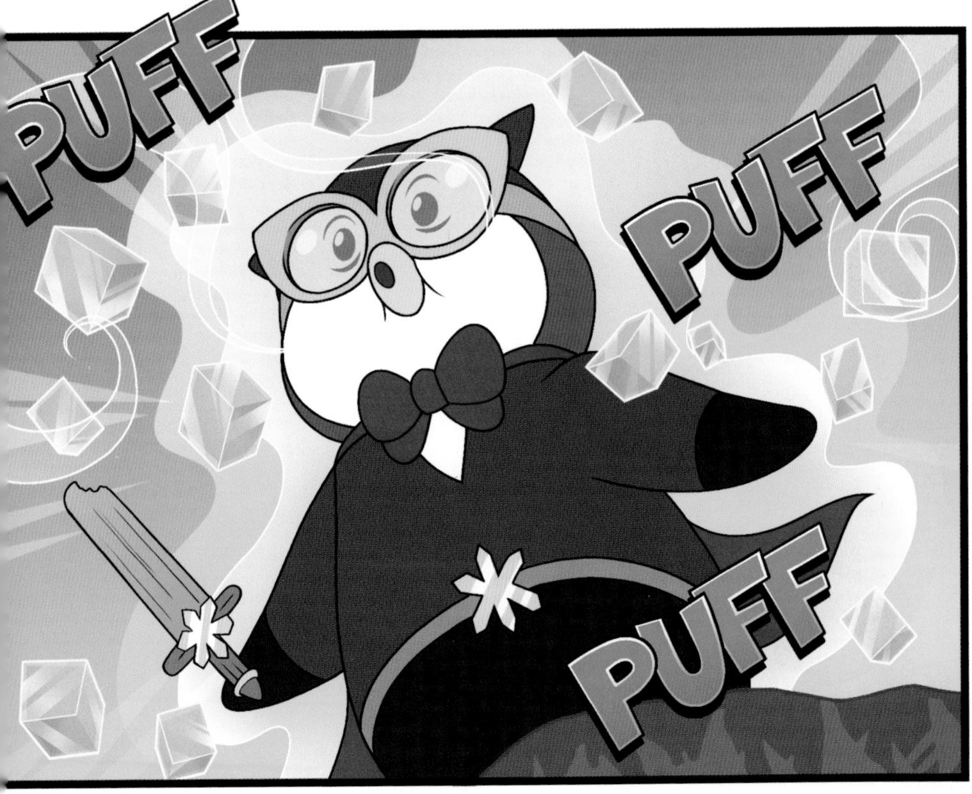
PUFF
PUFF
PUFF

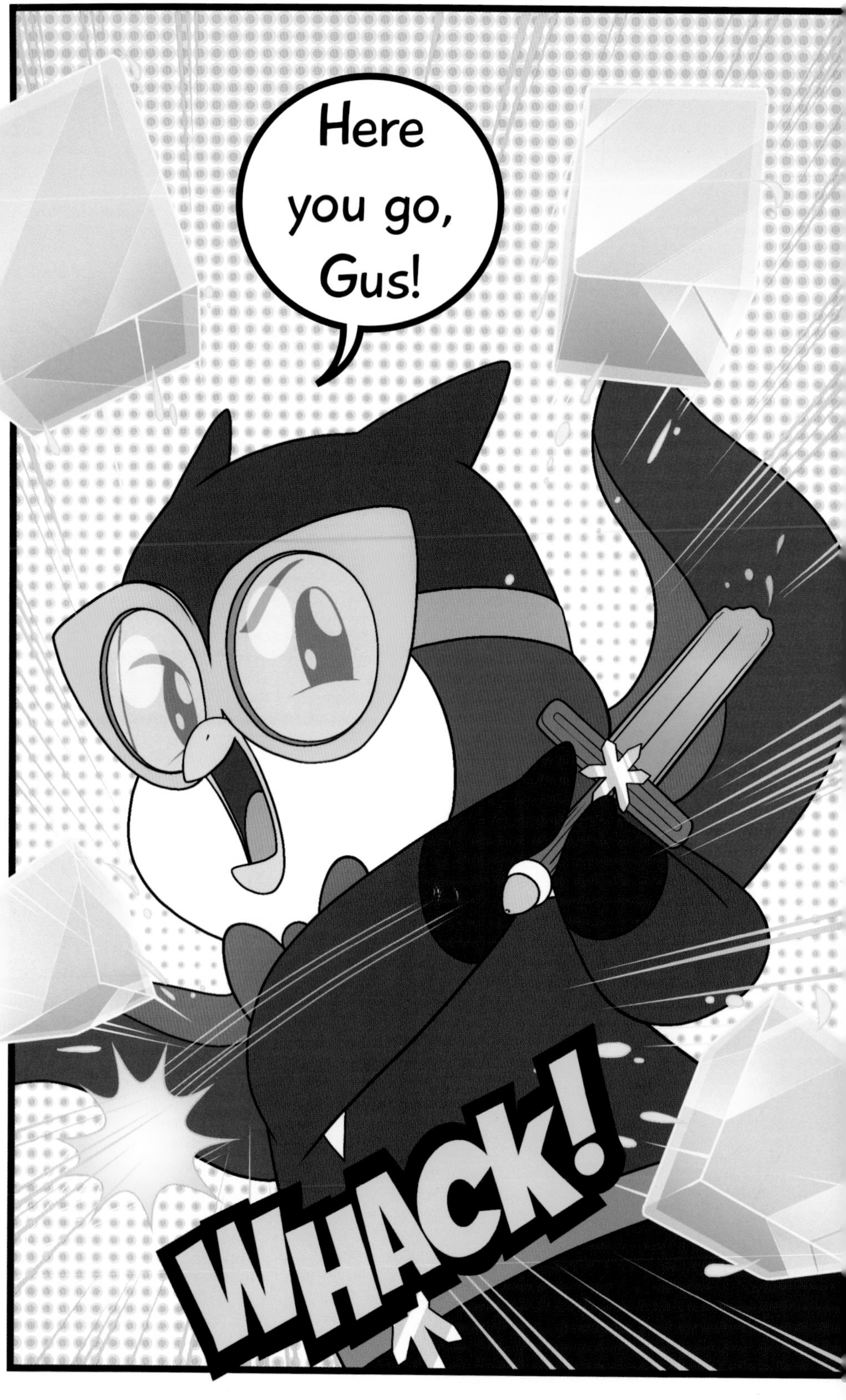
Here you go, Gus!
WHACK!

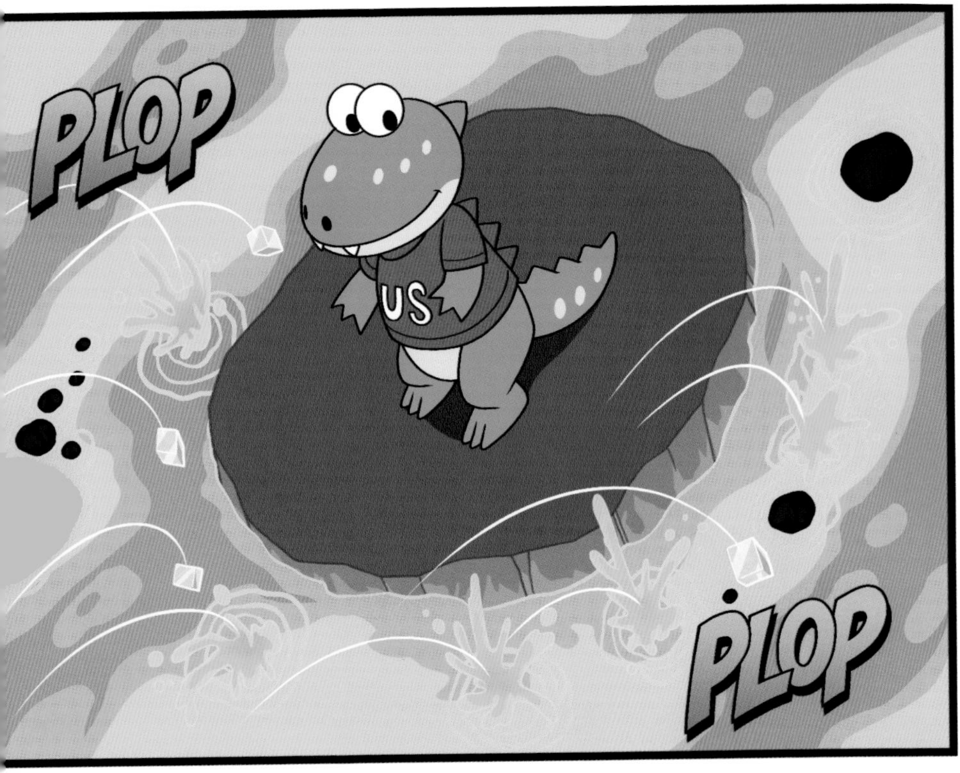
PLOP
PLOP

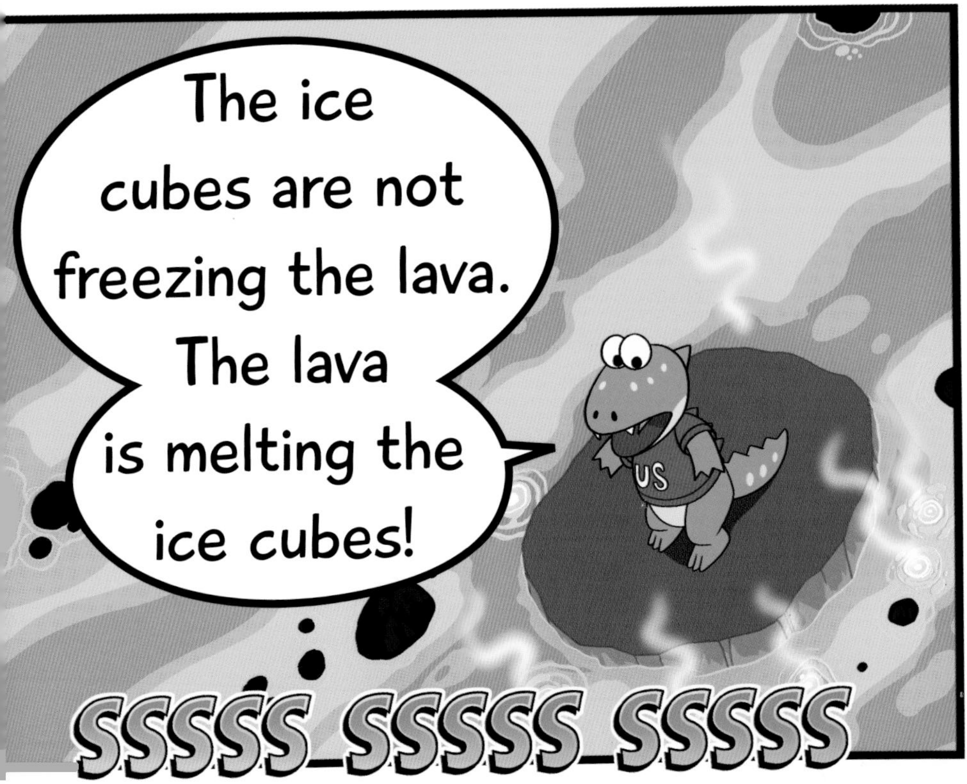
The ice cubes are not freezing the lava. The lava is melting the ice cubes!
SSSSS SSSSS SSSSS

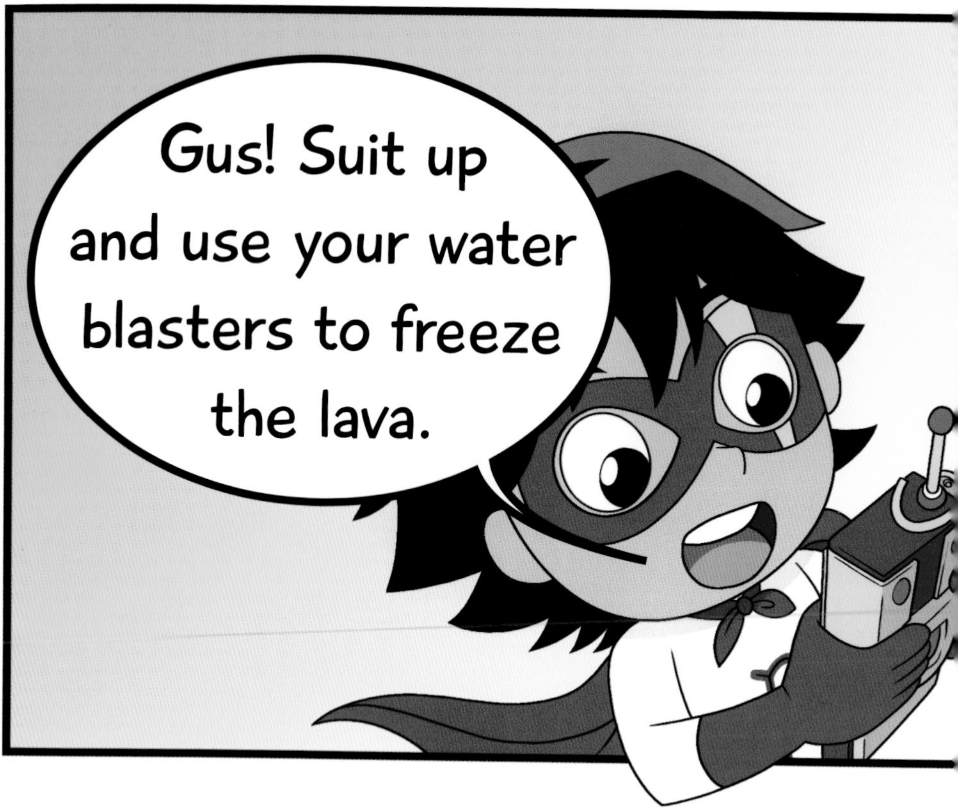
Gus! Suit up and use your water blasters to freeze the lava.

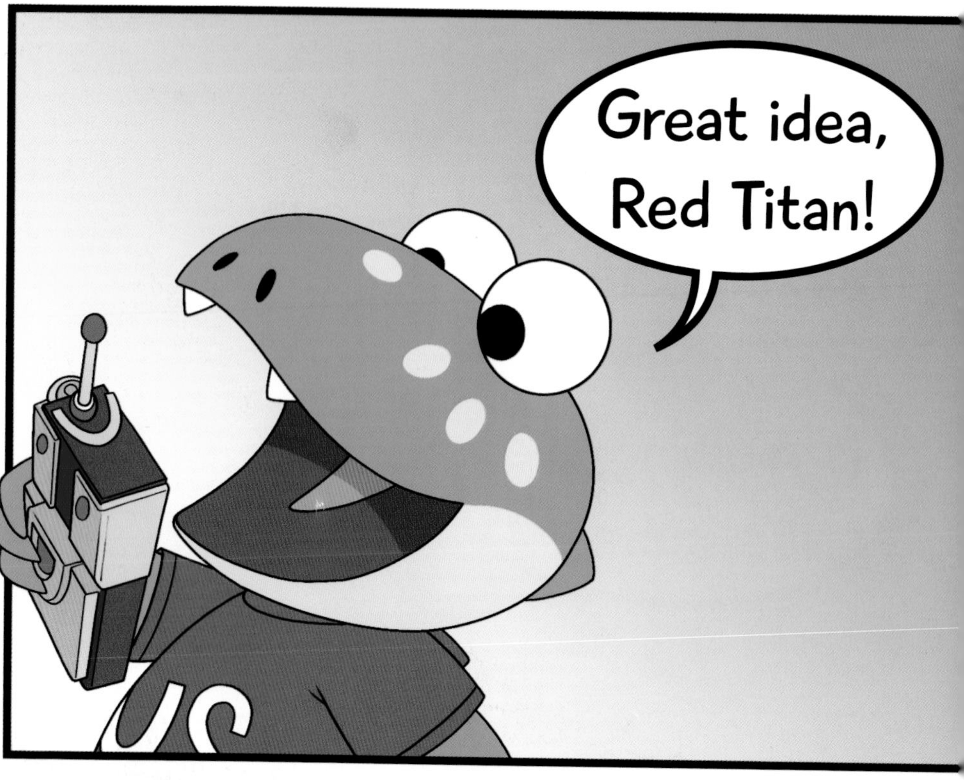
Great idea, Red Titan!

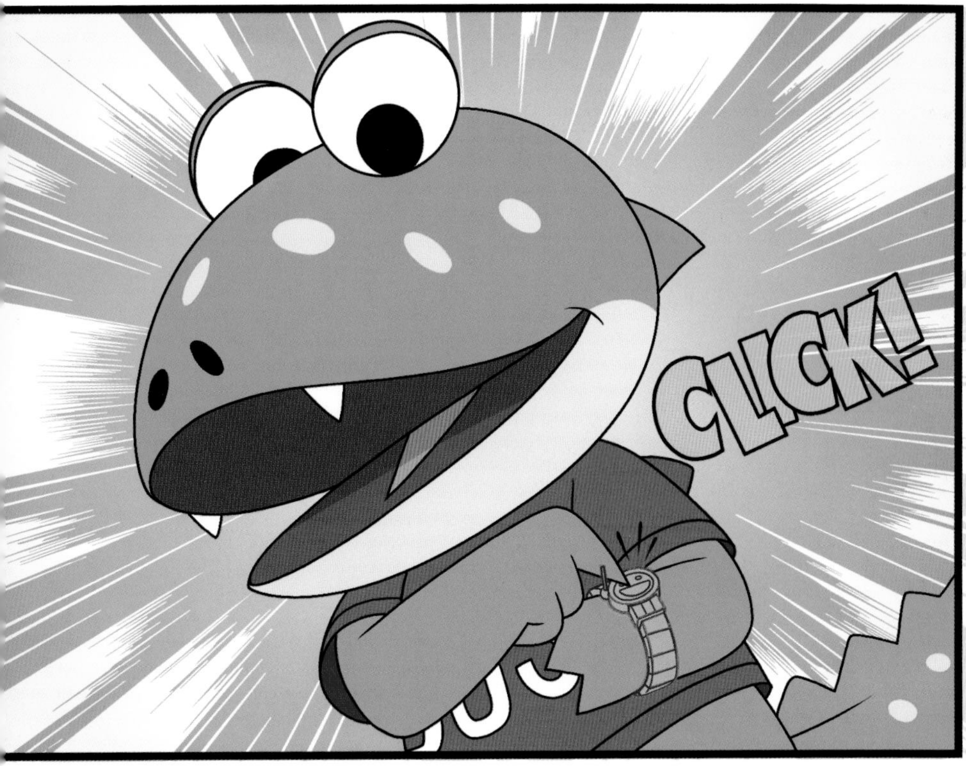
CLICK!
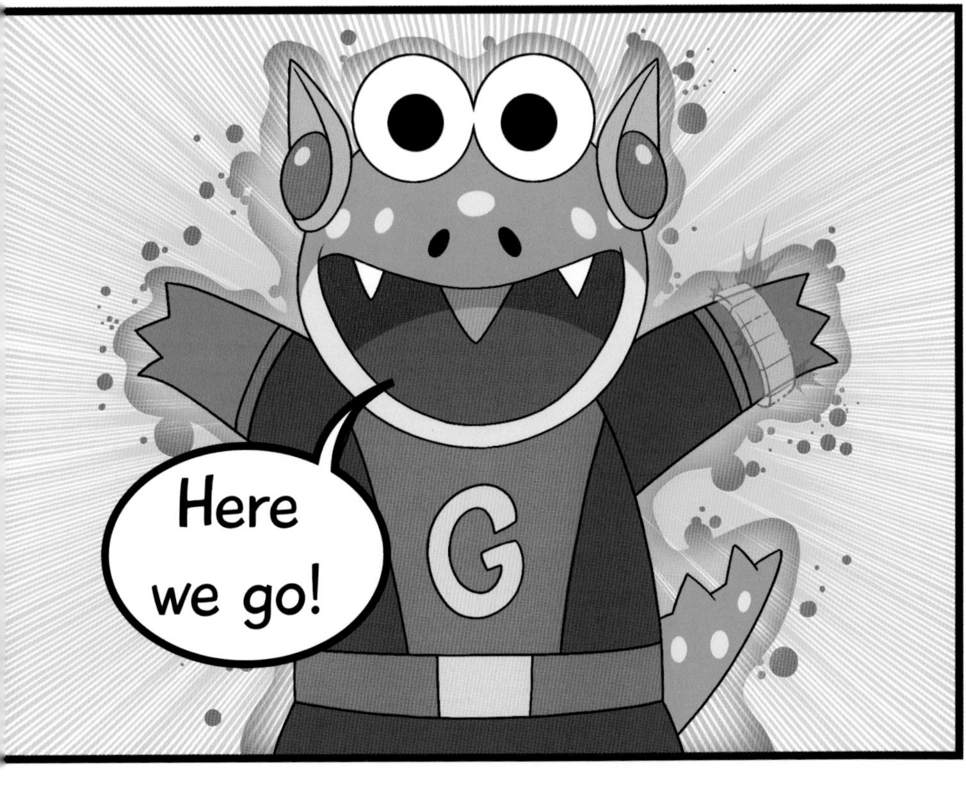
Here we go!

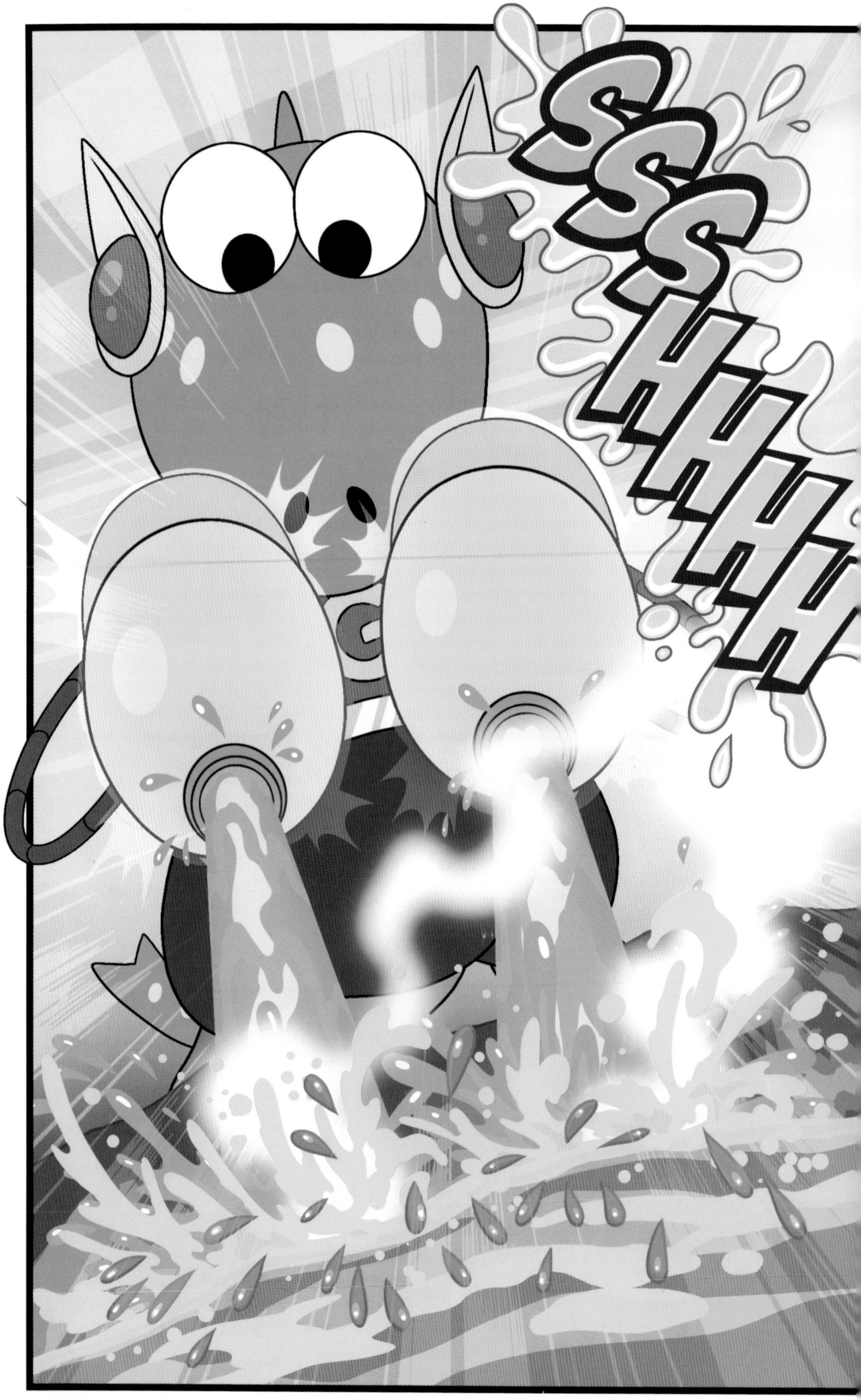
SSSHHHHH

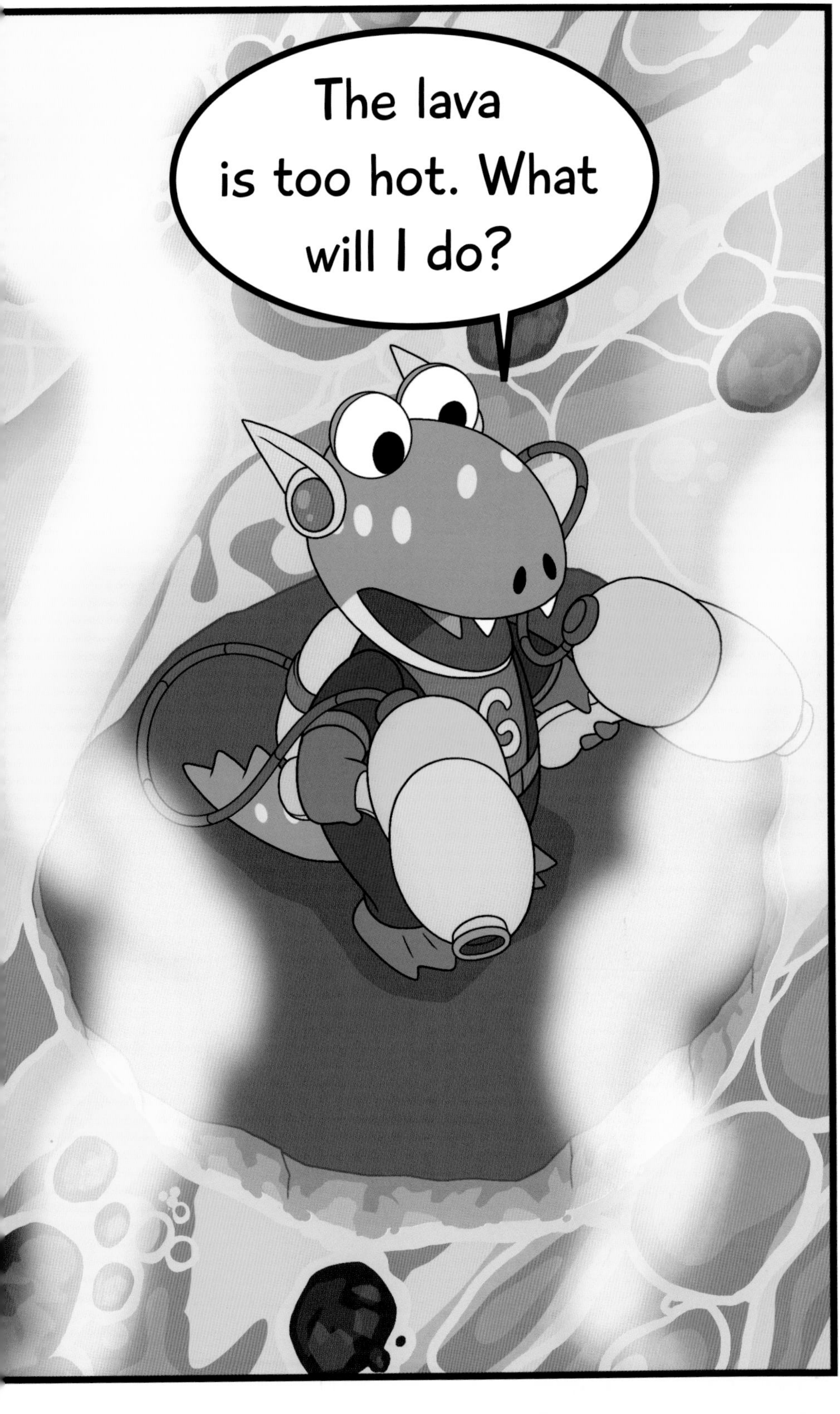
The lava is too hot. What will I do?

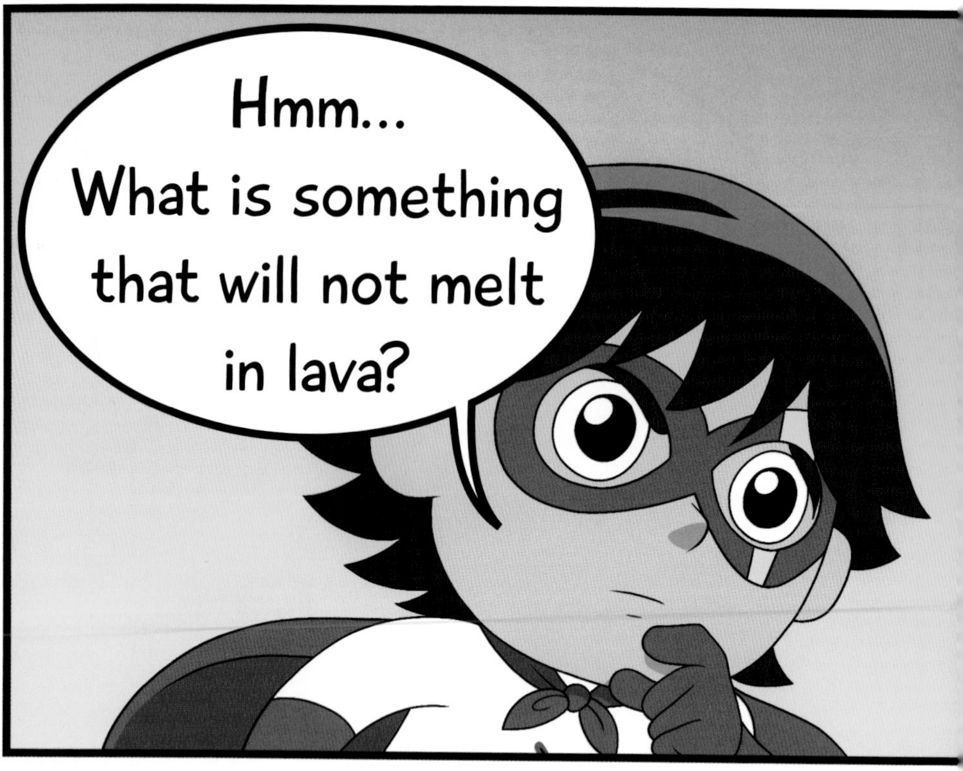
Hmm... What is something that will not melt in lava?

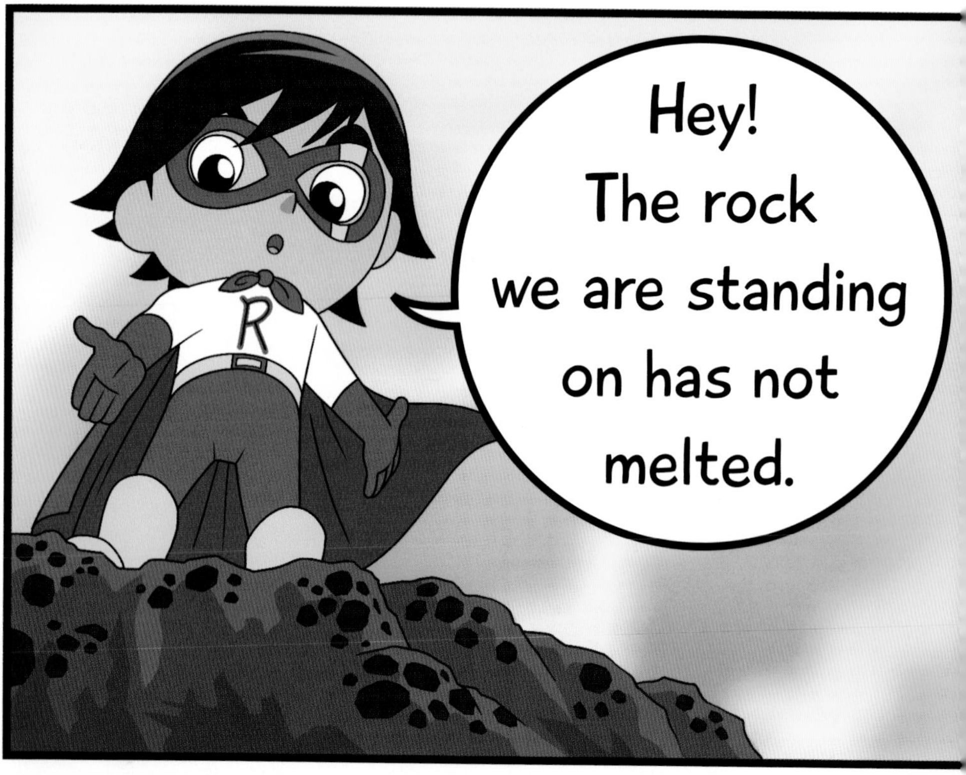
Hey! The rock we are standing on has not melted.

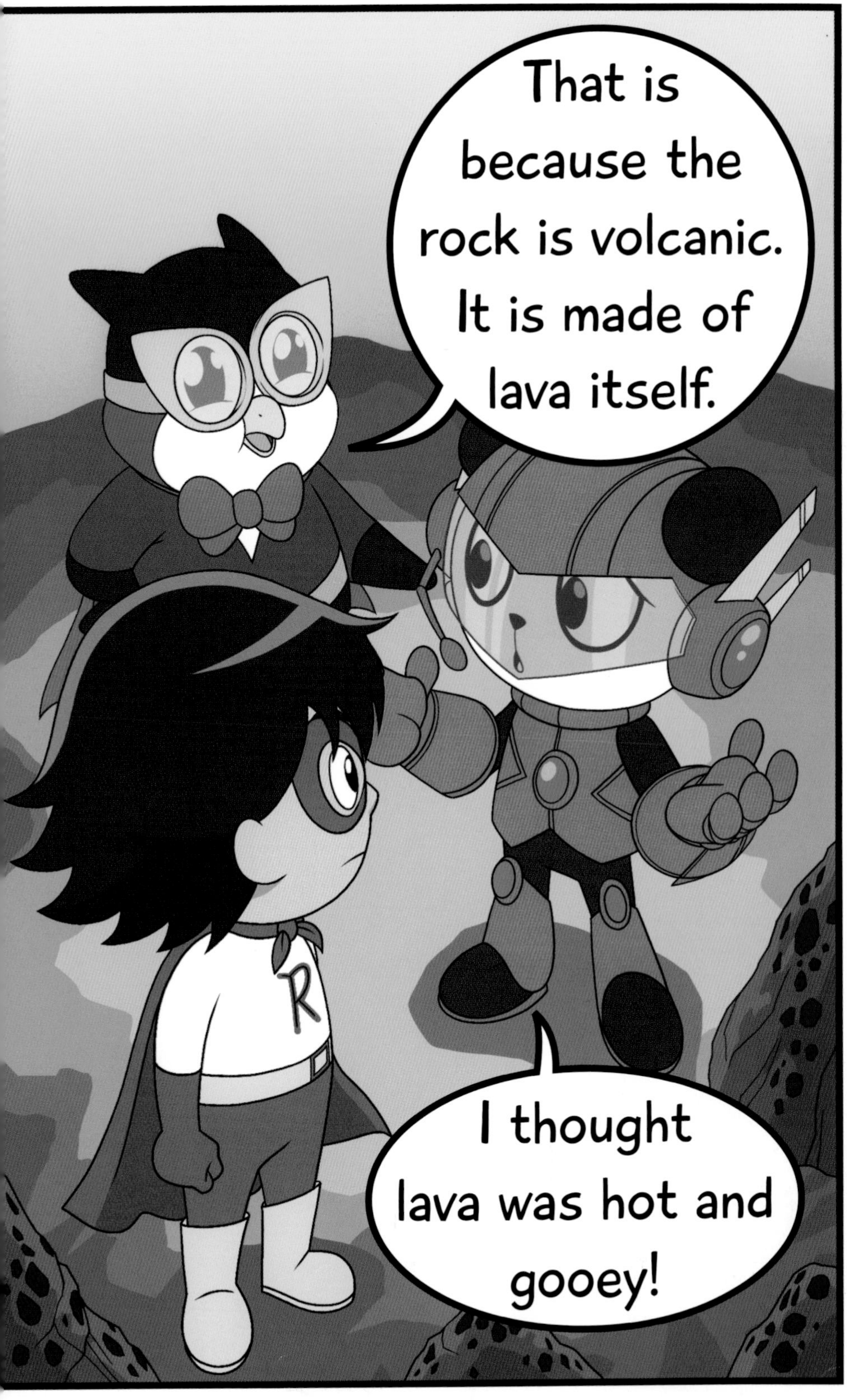
That is because the rock is volcanic. It is made of lava itself.
I thought lava was hot and gooey!

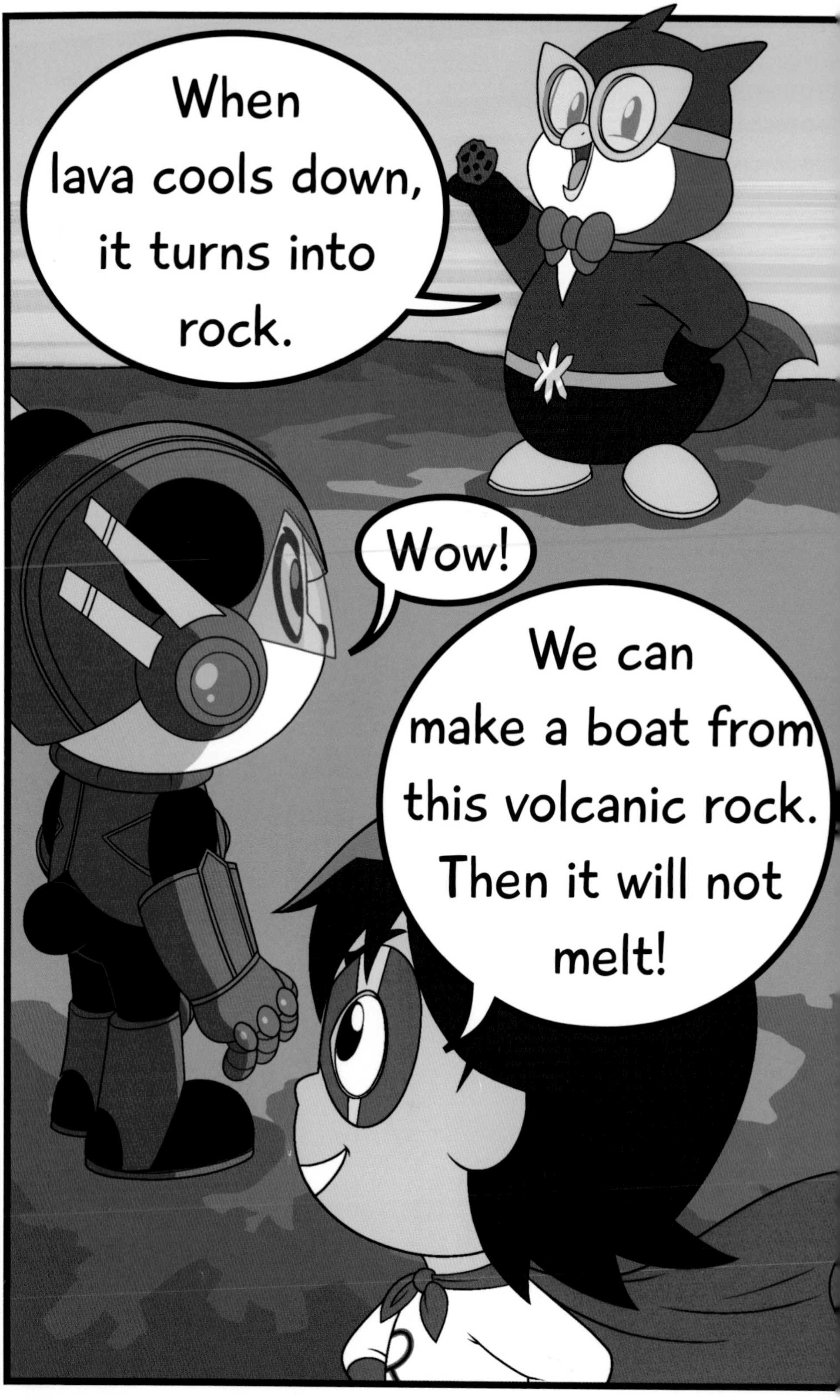
When lava cools down, it turns into rock.
Wow!
We can make a boat from this volcanic rock. Then it will not melt!

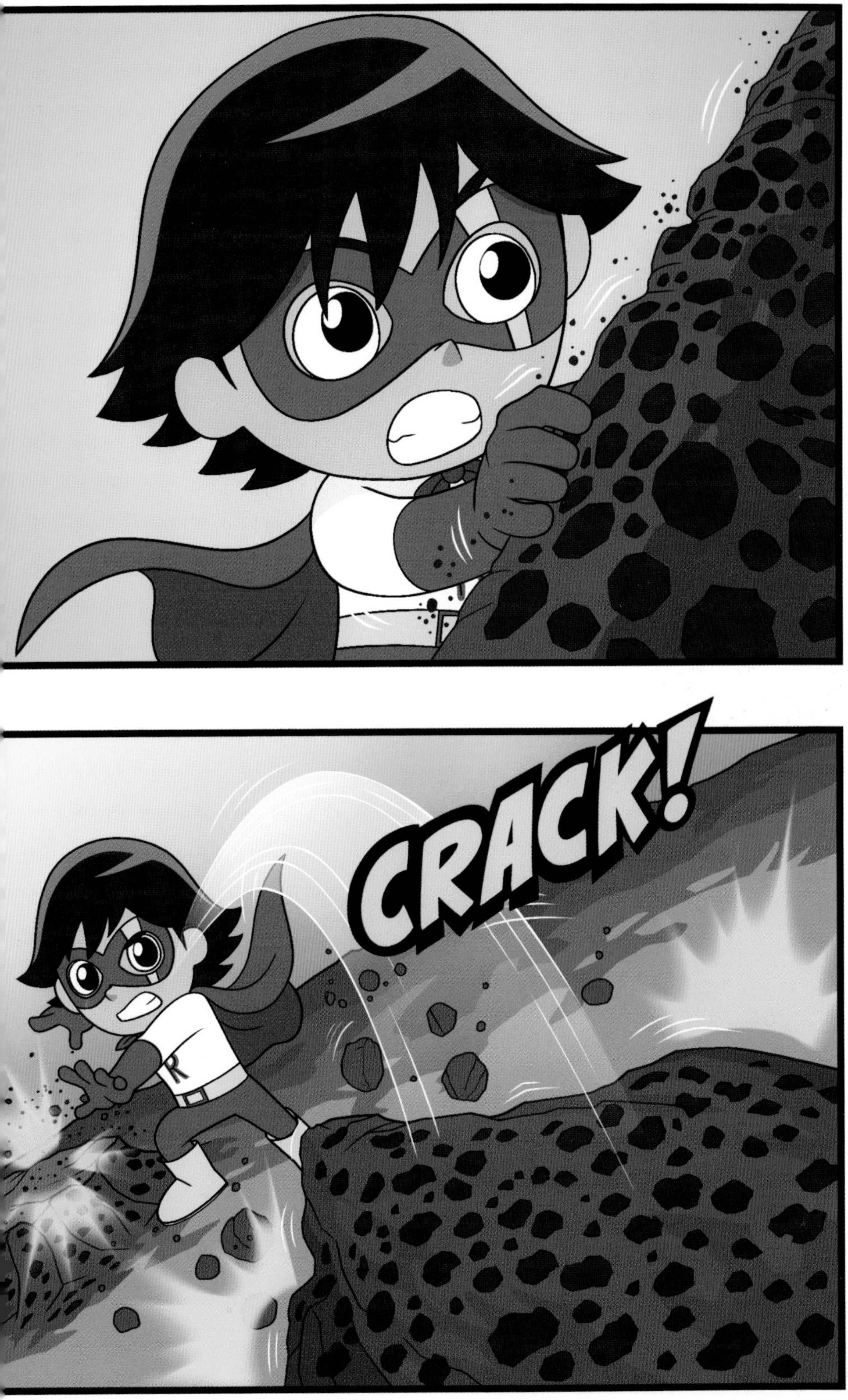
CRACK!

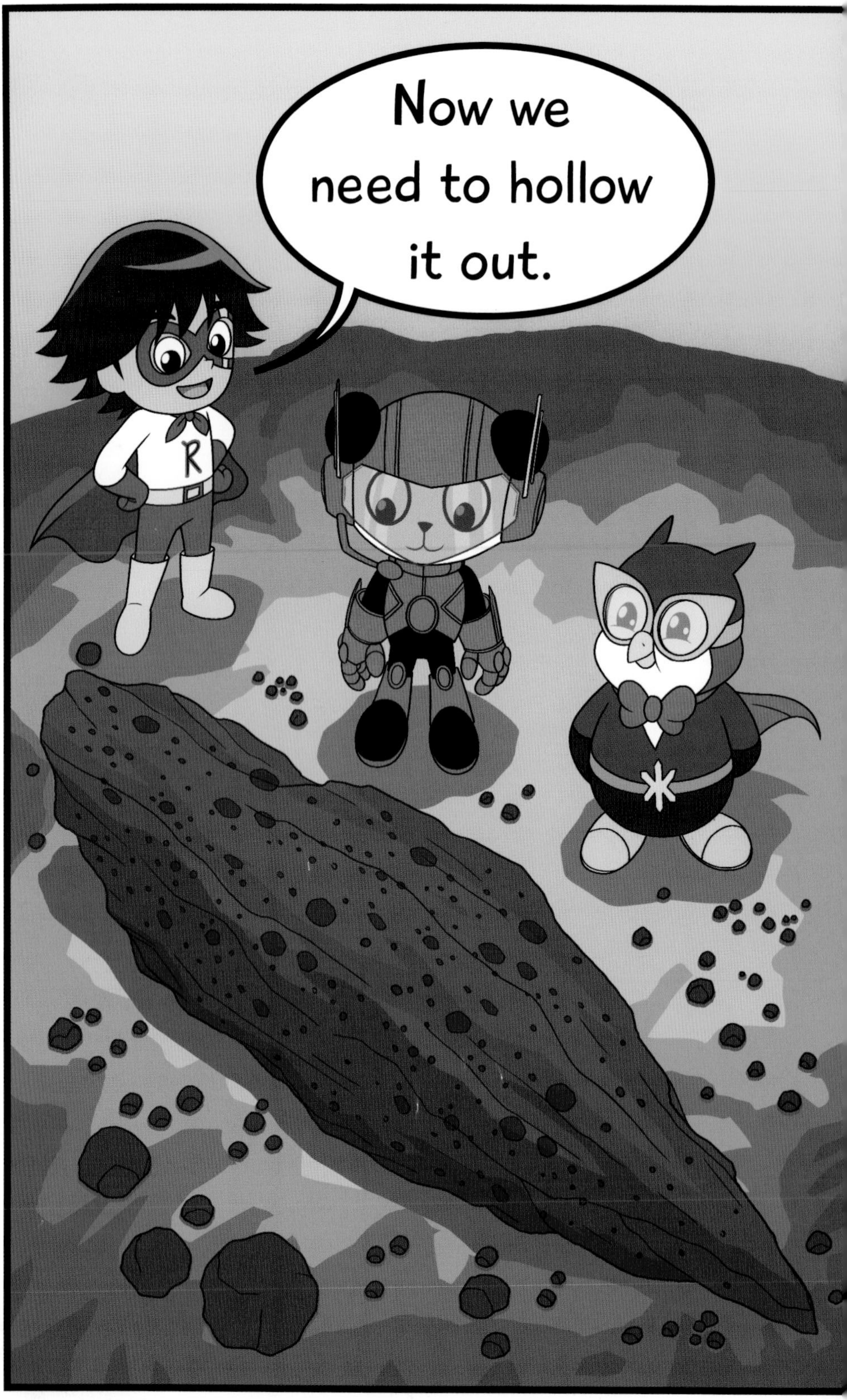
Now we need to hollow it out.
R

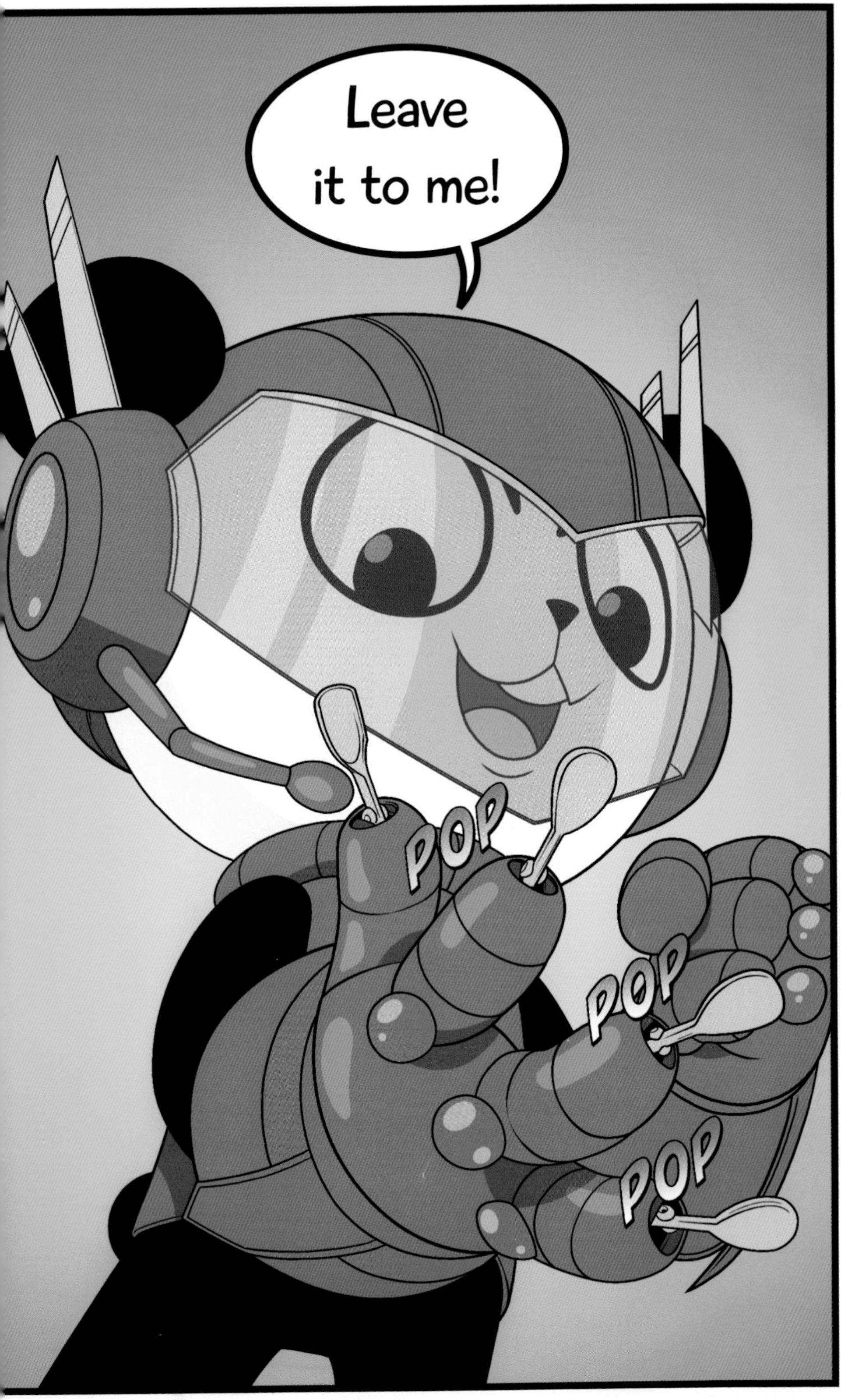
Leave
it to me!
POP
POP
POP

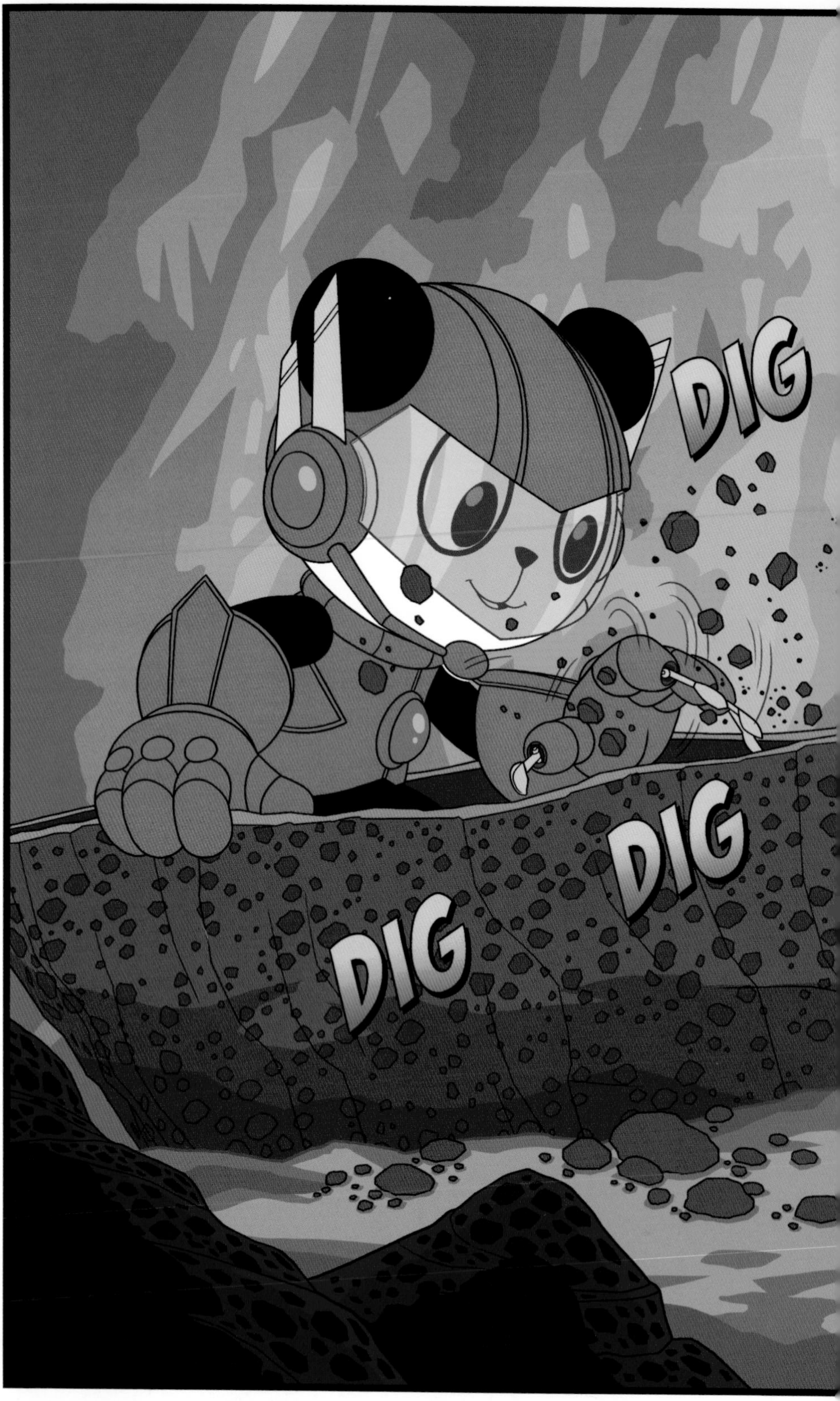
DIG
DIG
DIG

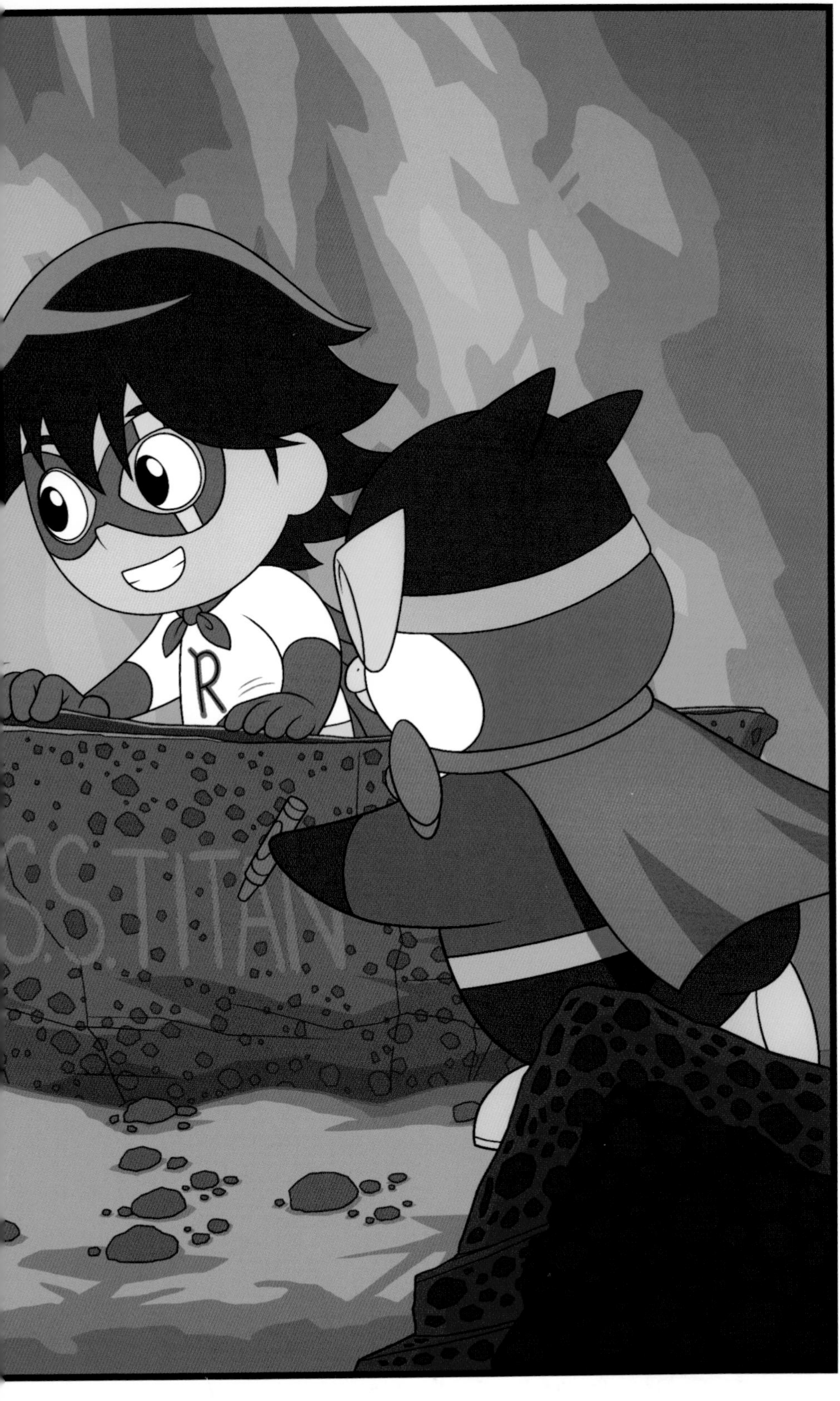
S.S.TITAN

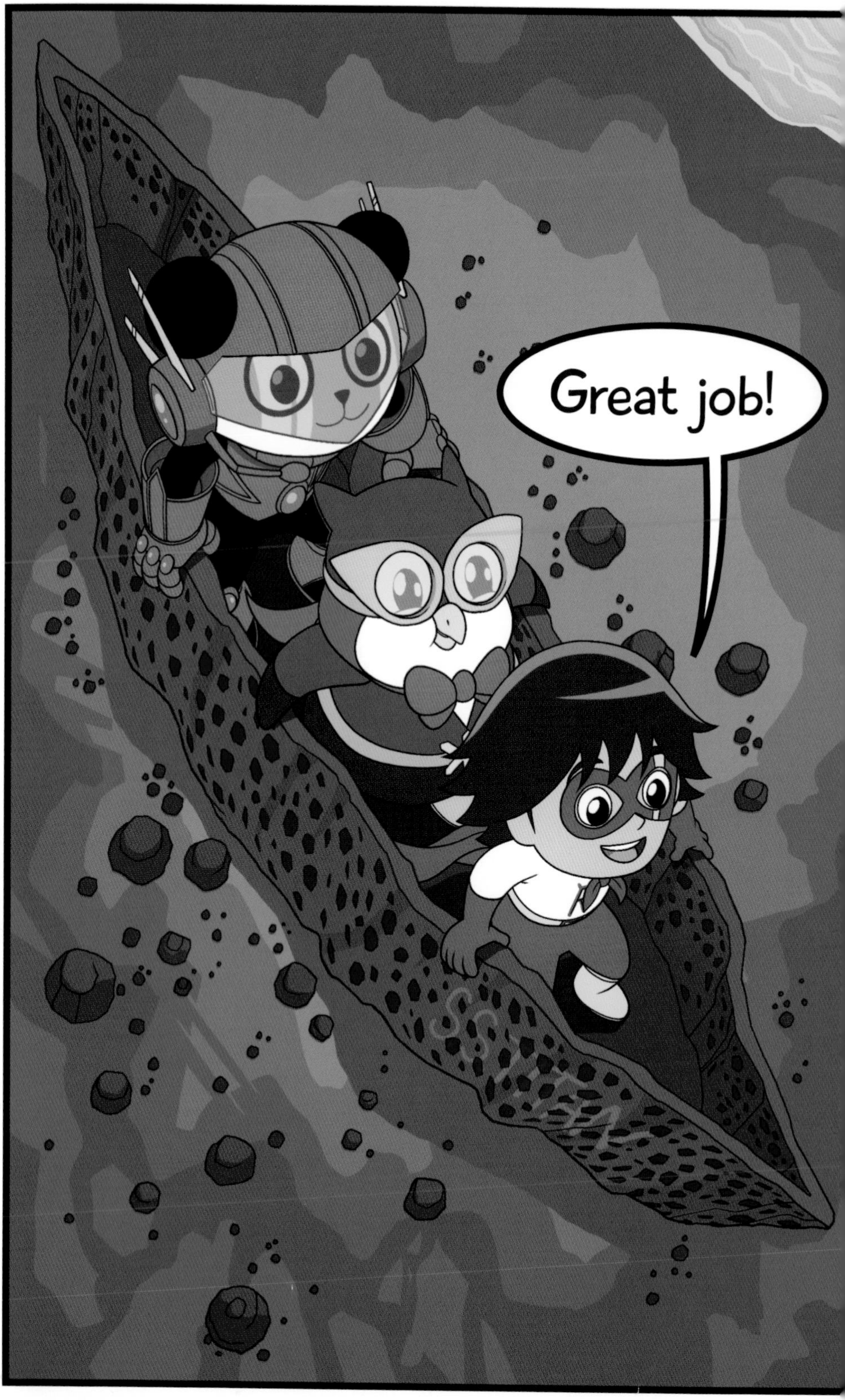
Great job!

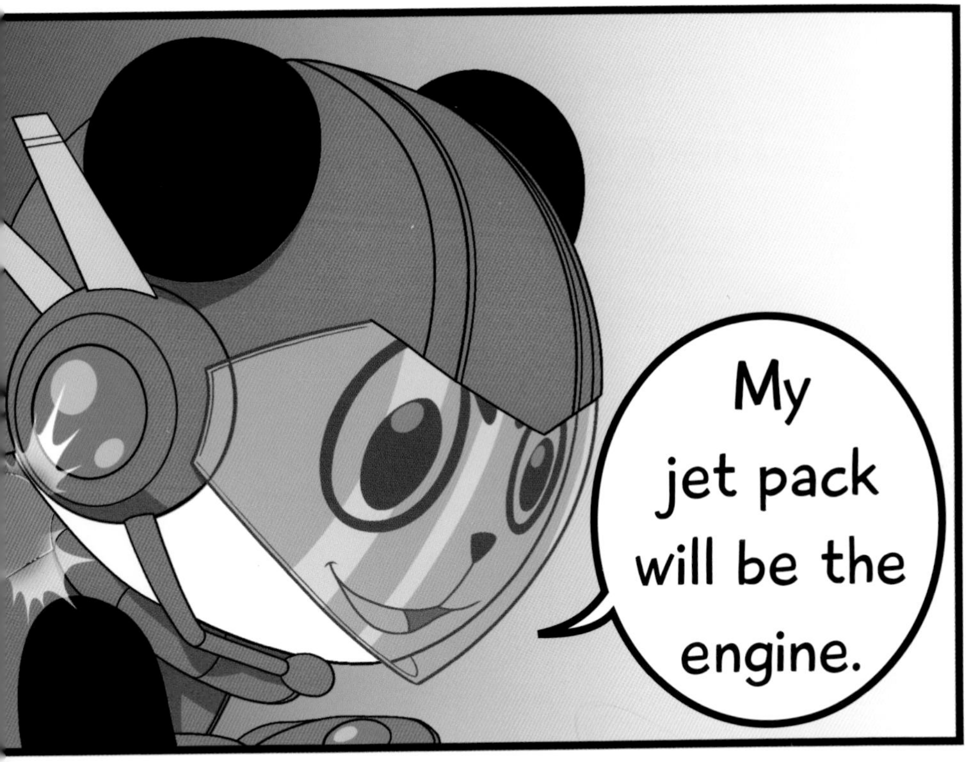
My jet pack will be the engine.

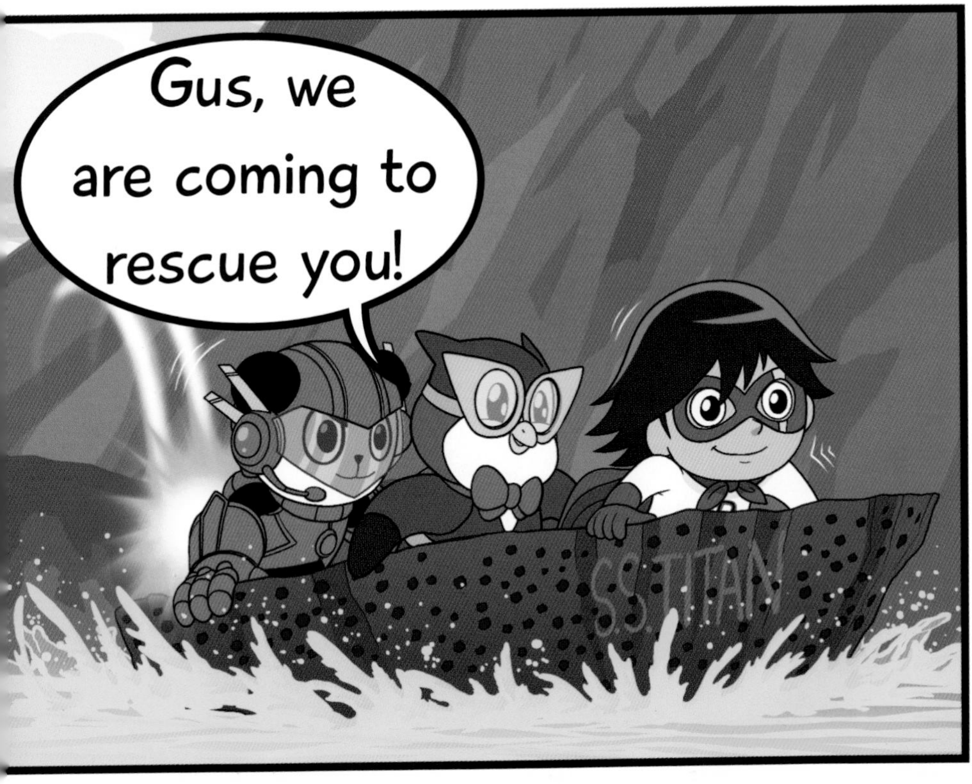
Gus, we are coming to rescue you!
S.S. TITAN

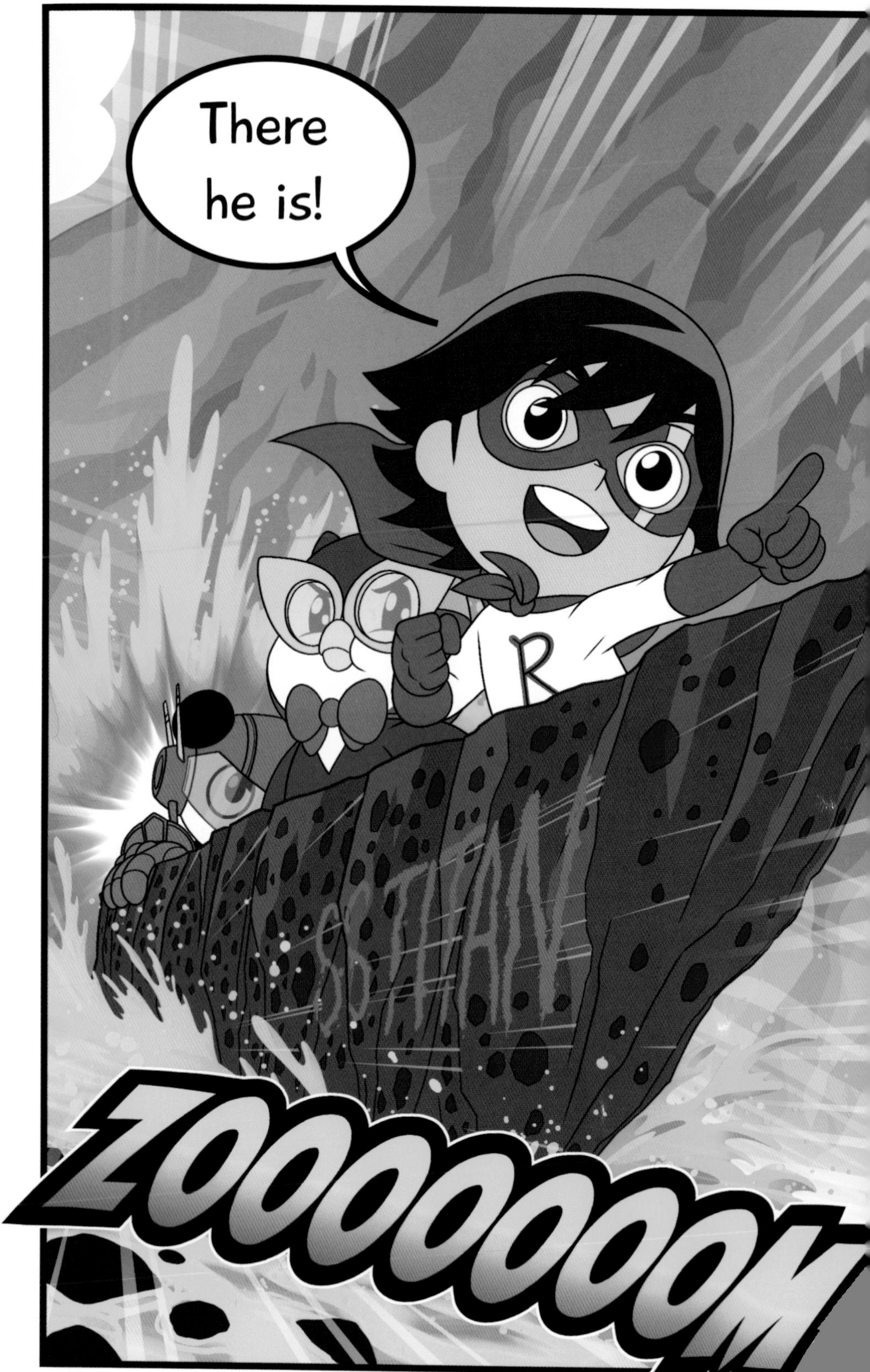
There he is!
ZOOOOOOOM

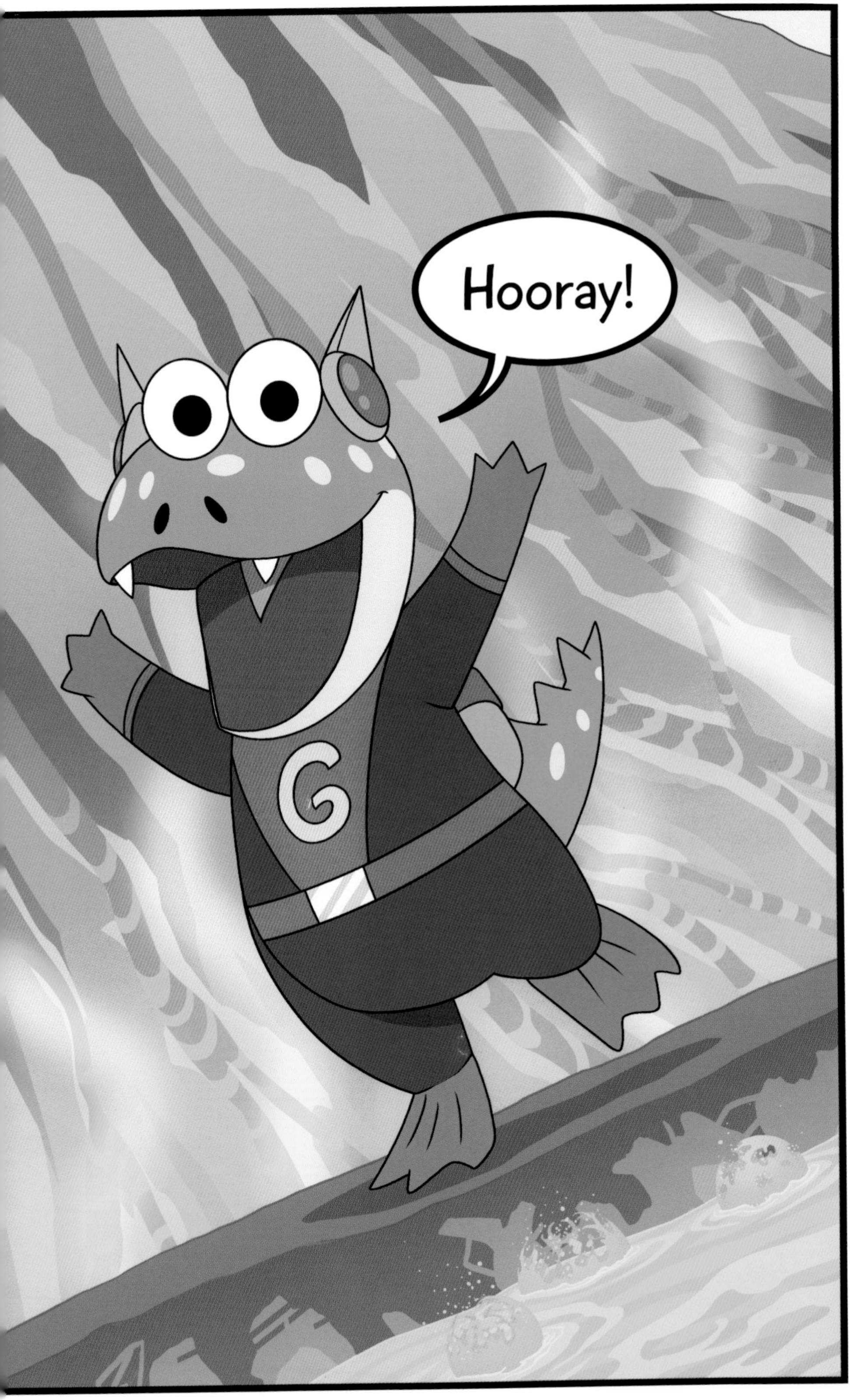
Hooray!

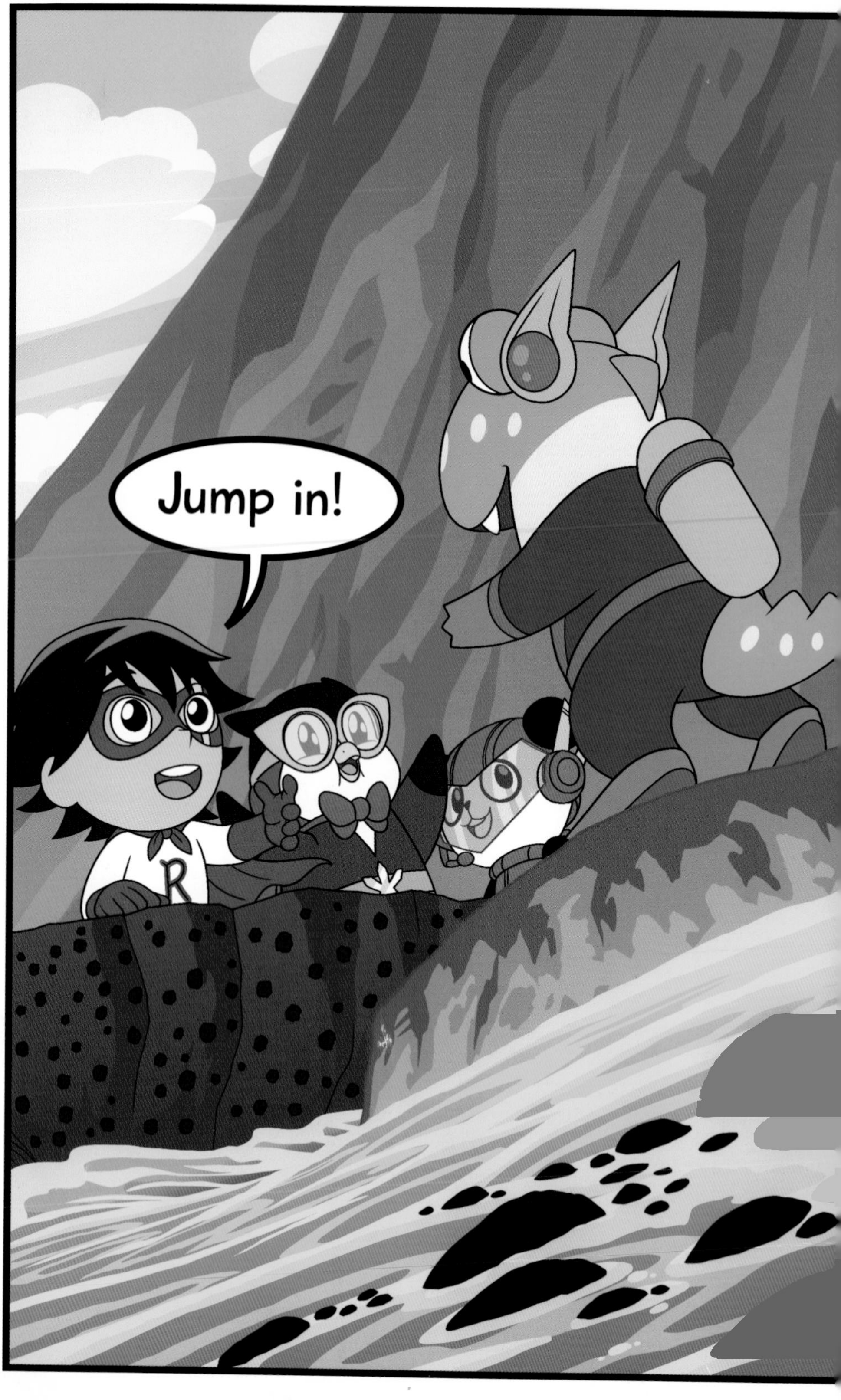
Jump in!

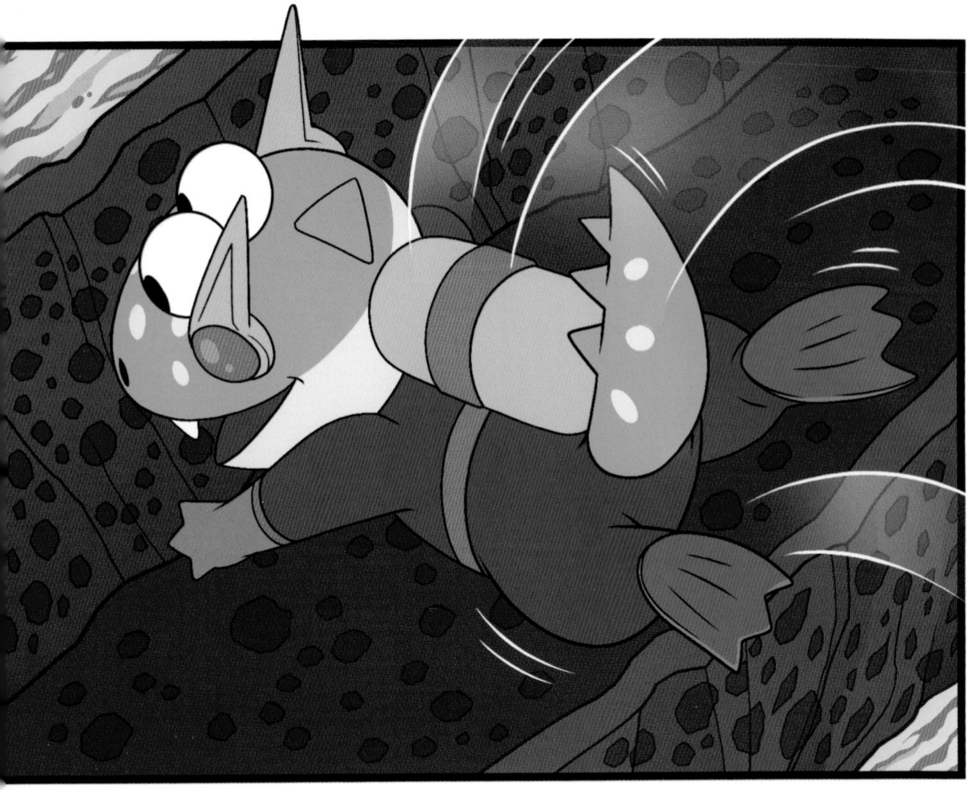

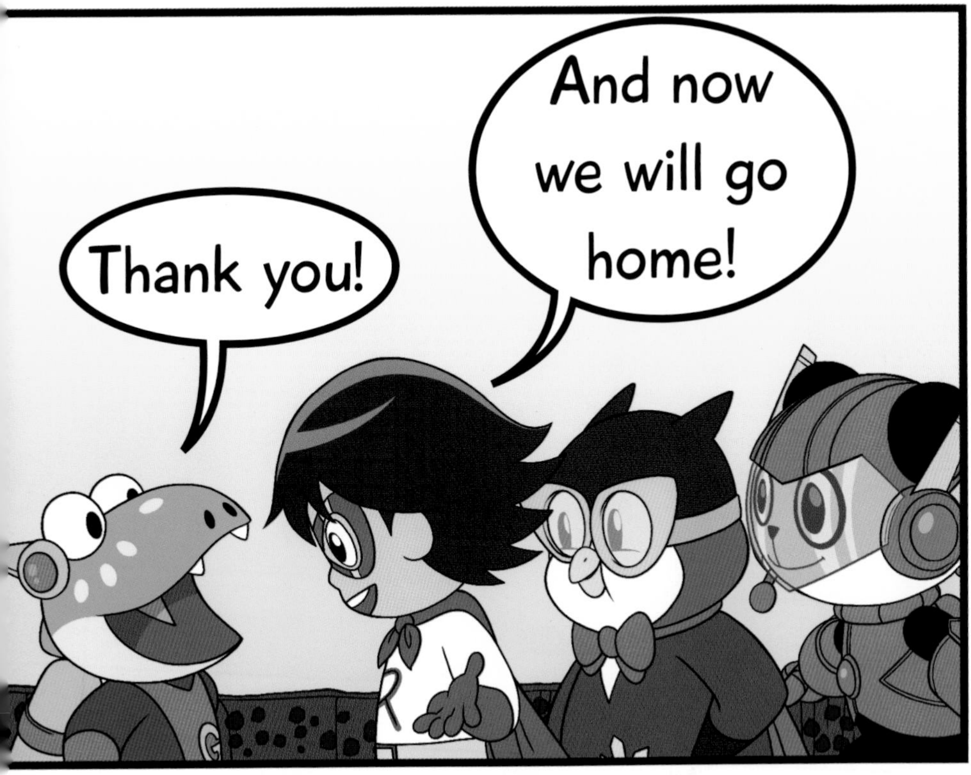
Thank you!
And now we will go home!

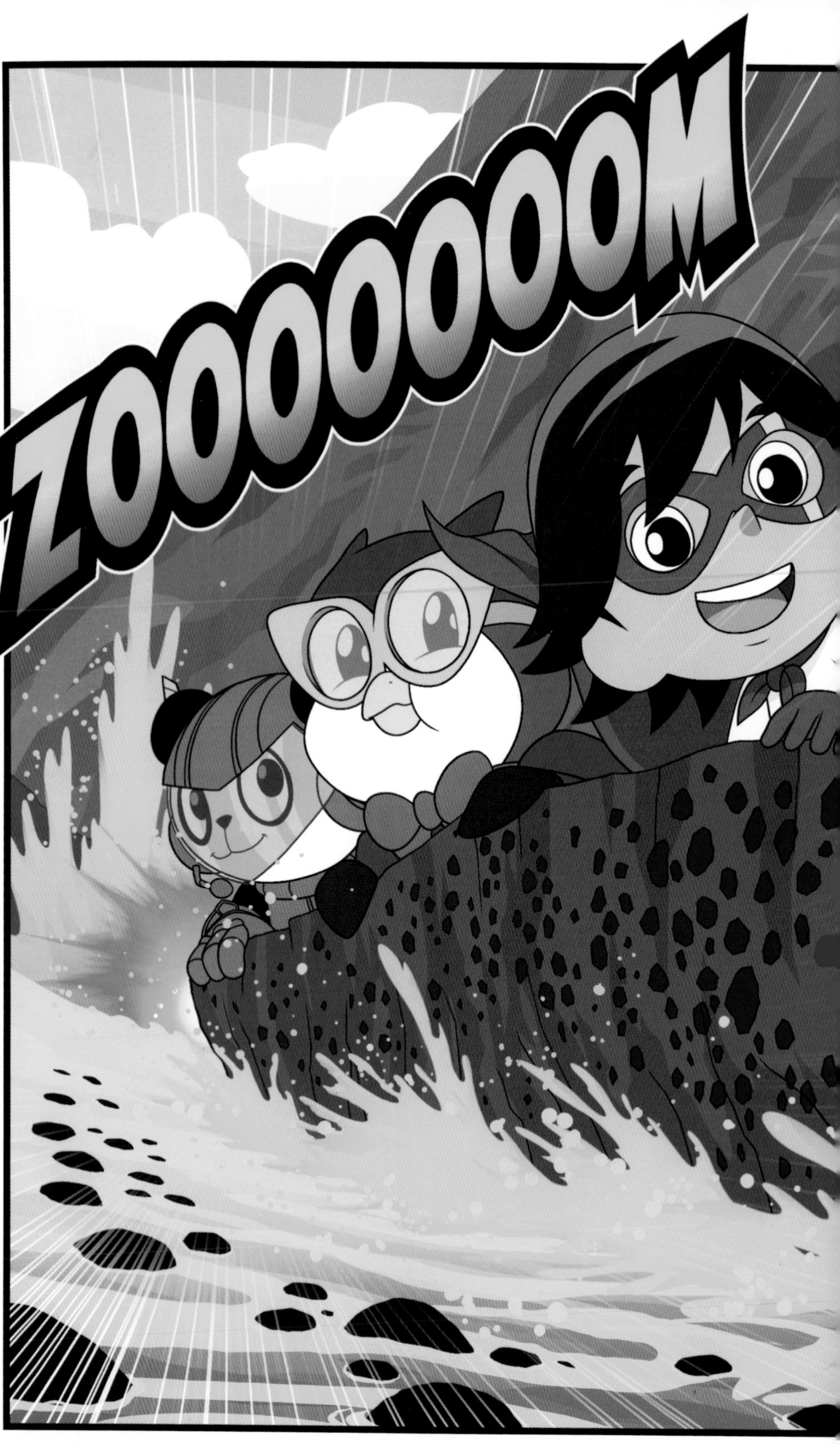
ZOOOOOOOOM

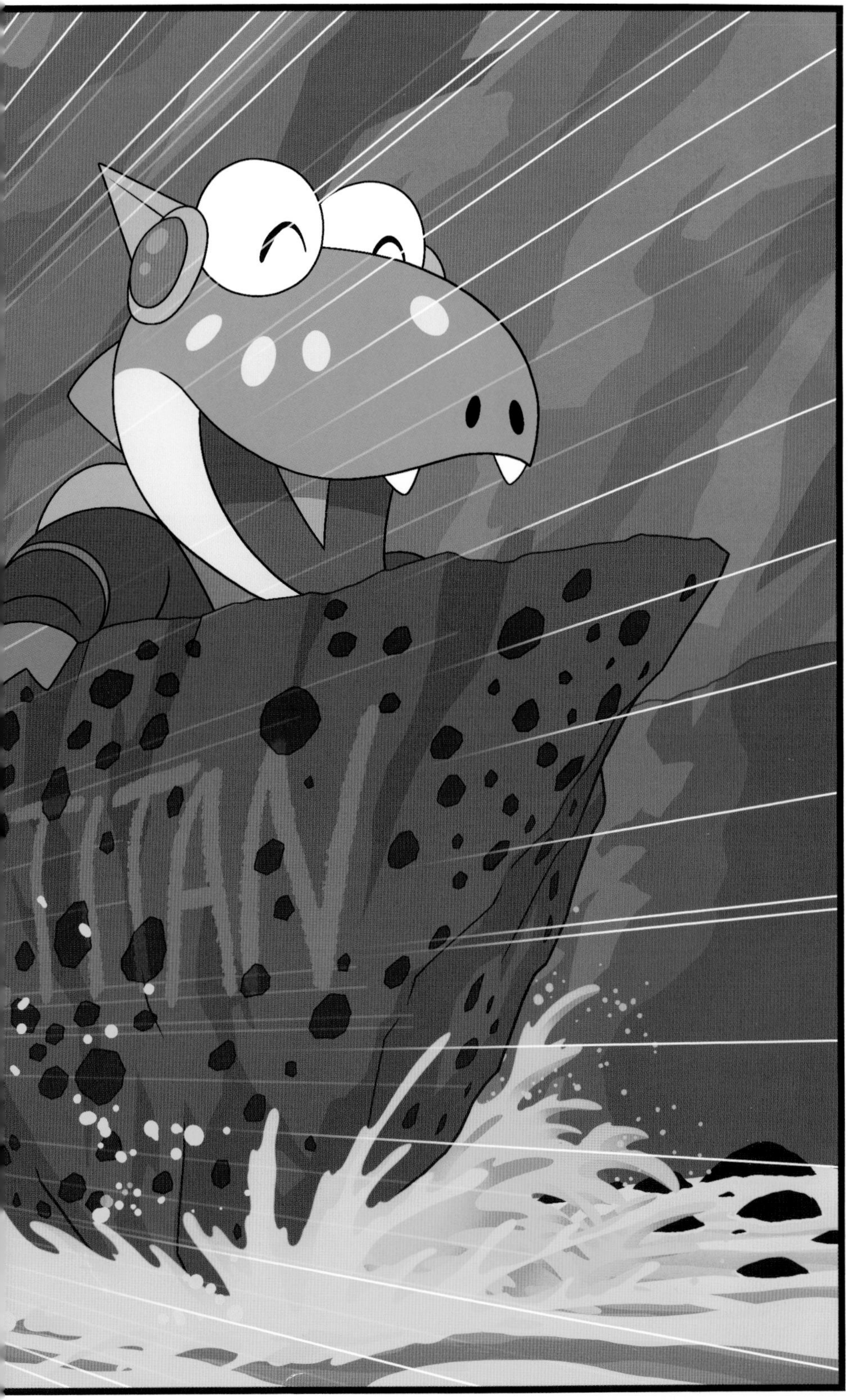
TITAN

The next day...

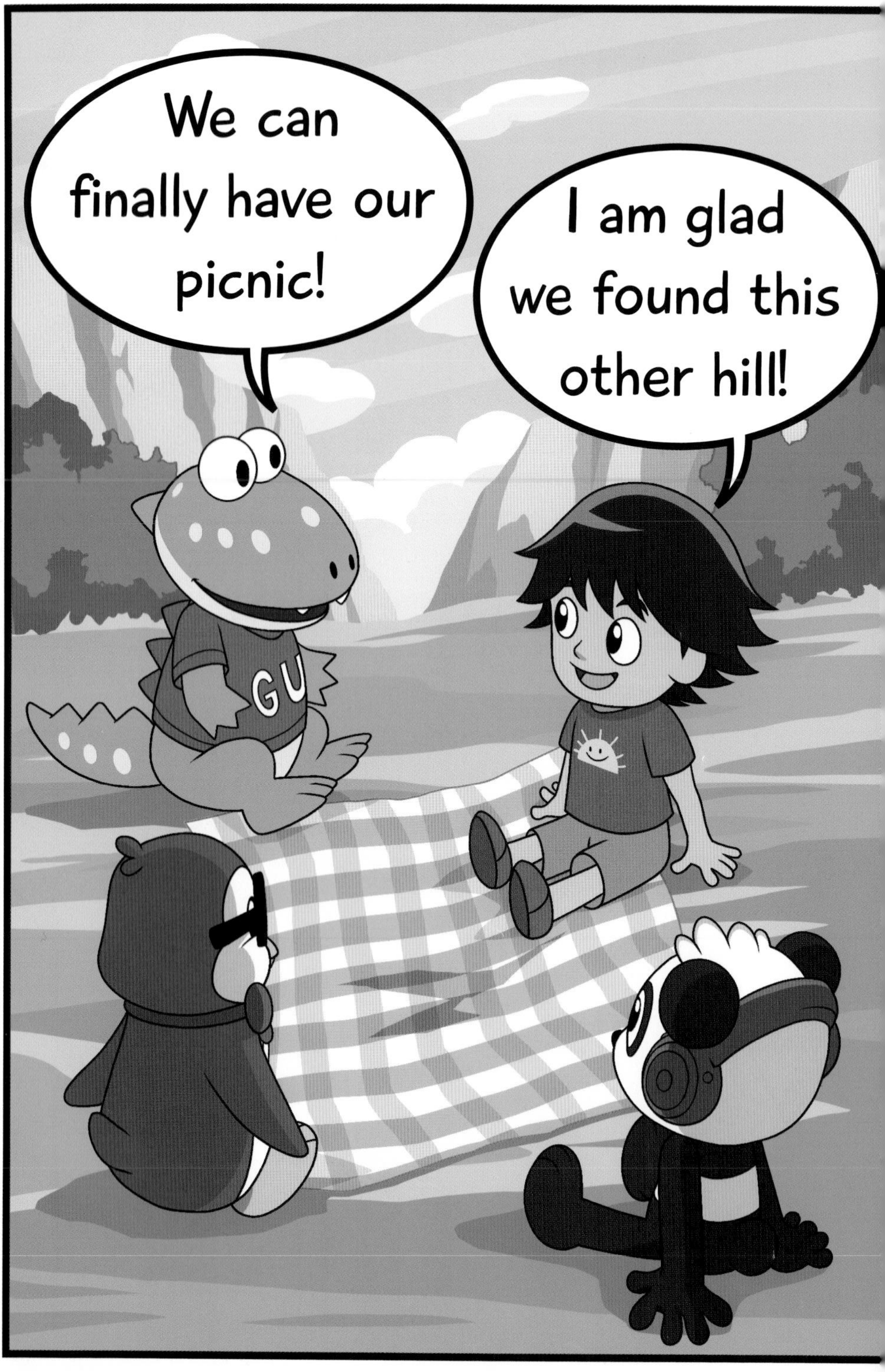
We can finally have our picnic!
I am glad we found this other hill!
GU

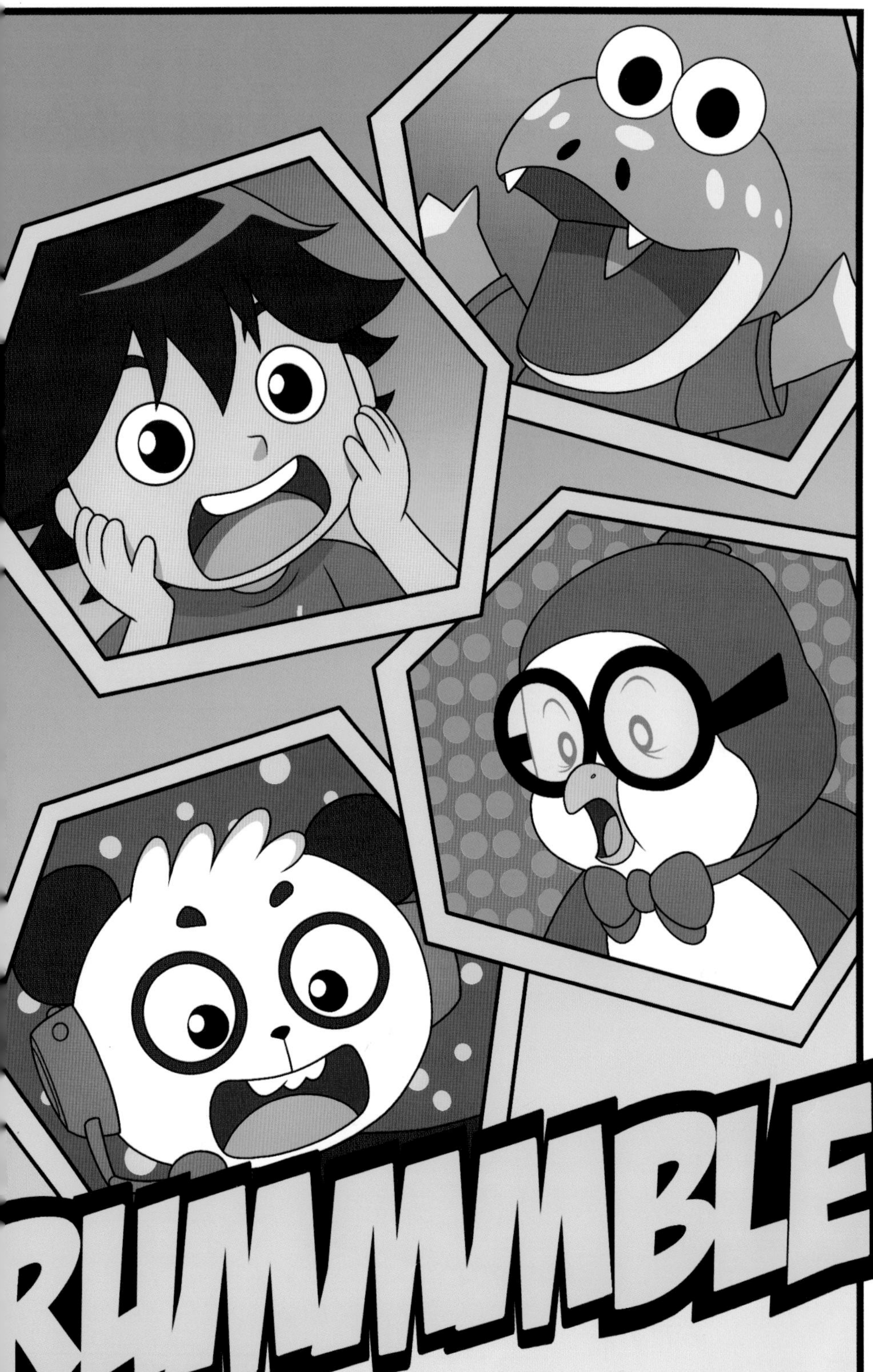
RUMMMBLE

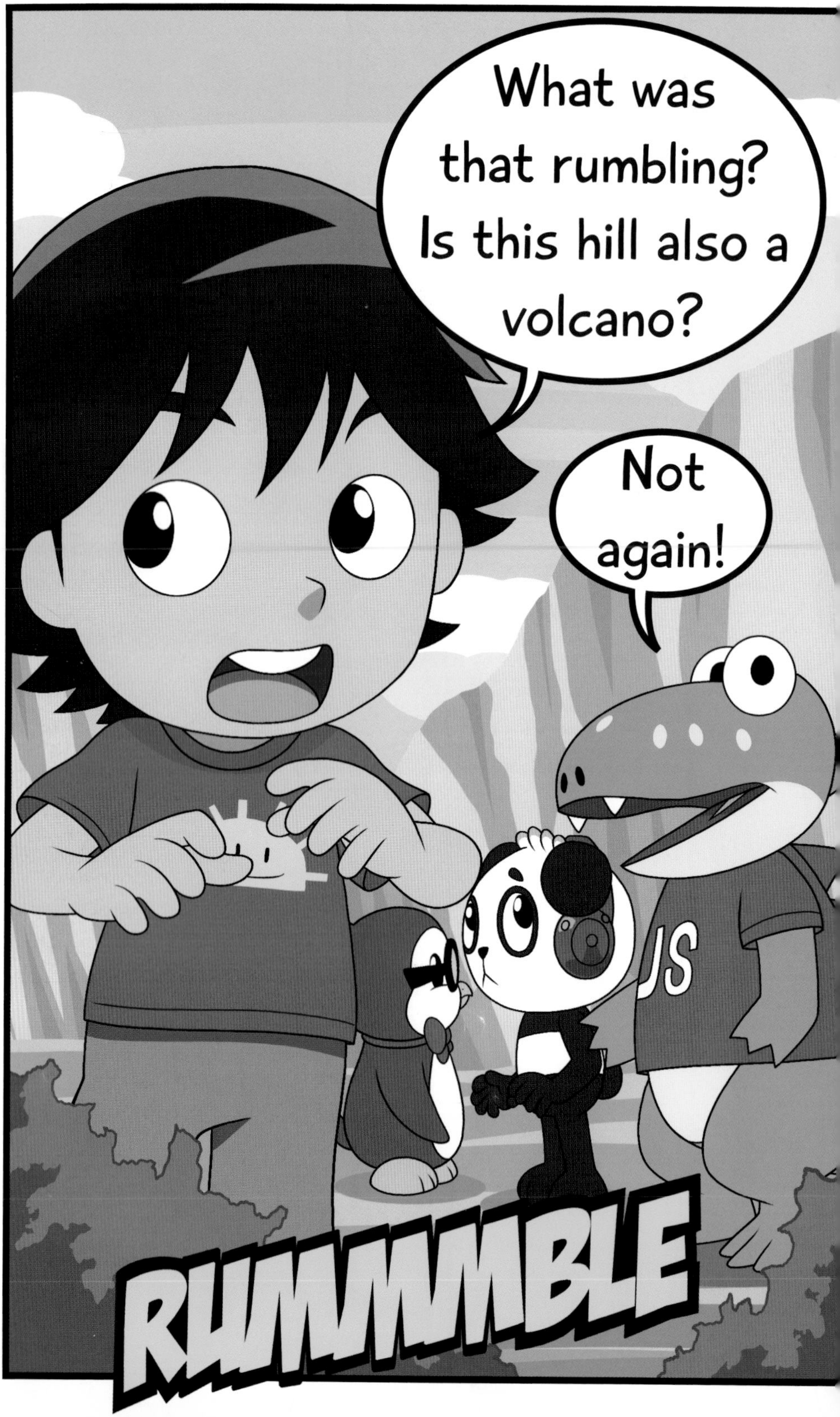
What was that rumbling? Is this hill also a volcano?
Not again!
RUMMMBLE

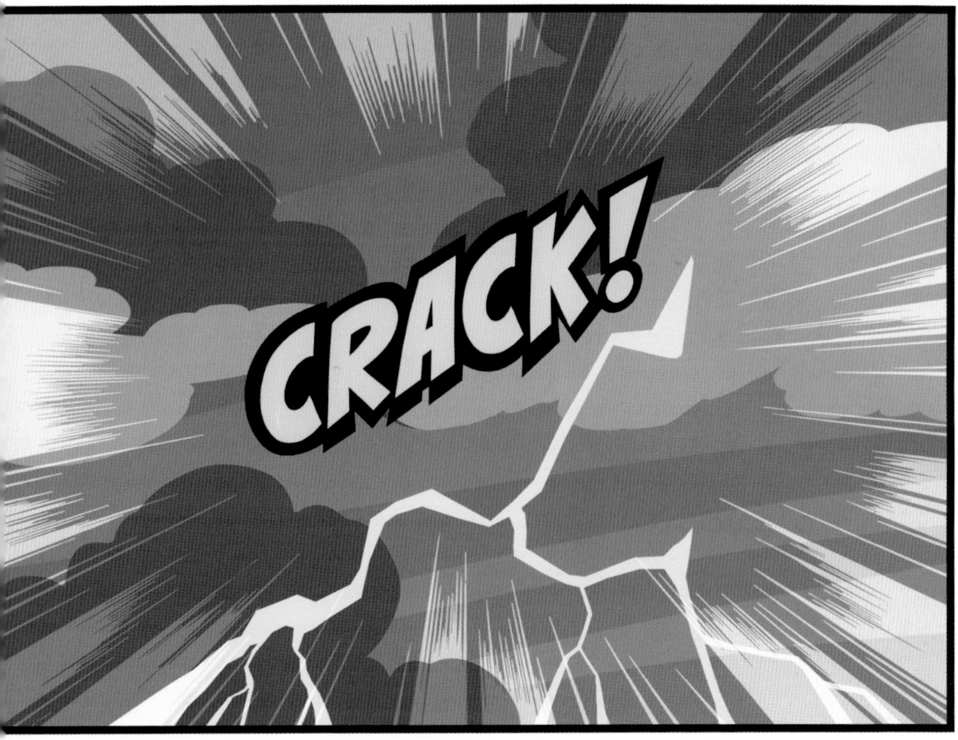
CRACK!

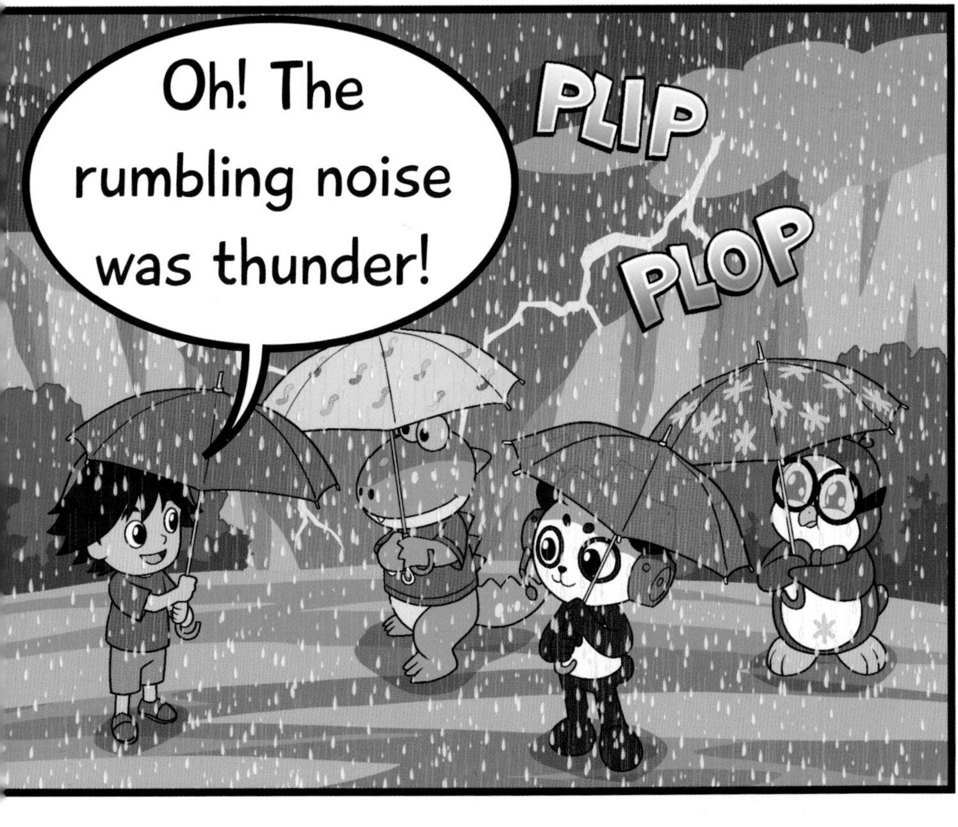
Oh! The rumbling noise was thunder!
PLIP
PLOP

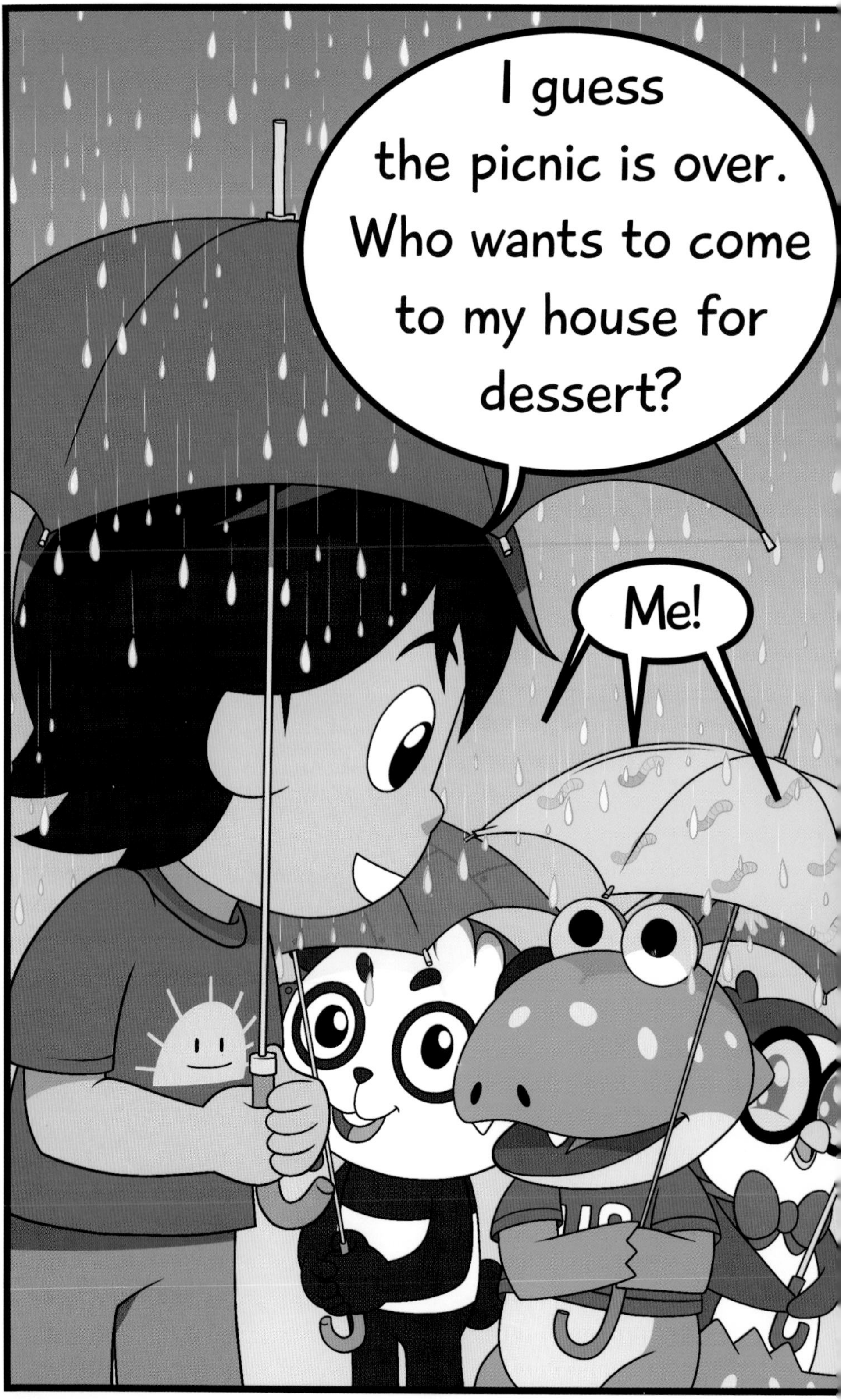
I guess the picnic is over. Who wants to come to my house for dessert?
Me!